Typewriter Pub, an imprint of Blvnp Incorporated
A Nevada Corporation
1887 Whitney Mesa DR #2002
Henderson, NV 89014
www.typewriterpub.com/info@typewriterpub.com

ISBN: 978-1-64434-102-5

DISCLAIMER
This book is a work of fiction. The characters, incidents, and dialogue are drawn from the author's imagination and are not to be construed as real. While references might be made to actual historical events or existing locations, the names, characters, places, and incidents are either products of the author's imagination or are used fictitiously, and any resemblance to actual persons living or dead, business establishments, events or locales is entirely coincidental.

GW00670487

SWEET REVENGE

FLORA MCCONNELL

type writer pub

To my family,
for always being so supportive with my writing ambitions.

FREE DOWNLOAD

Get these freebies when you sign up for the
author's mailing list!

bit.ly/FloraMcConnellWEB

ONE

"Move, fat ass!" A loud voice echoes as I am pushed face first into the grimy blue lockers. My fat cheeks slam against the cold blue surface and splay out like an ice cream dropped on the ground. I wince and let out a groan of pain.

Nothing out of the ordinary though, being bullied is an everyday occurrence for people like me. By that, I mean people who are overweight.

Fat.

I push myself away from the lockers and shrug my hoodie back onto my shoulders, turning around to see the retreating figure of my tormenter. A mop of blond hair turns around to look at me, a smile etched on his face. It's Lucas Keith, one of the most attractive boys on this earth whose mission is to make my world a living hell.

Sometimes, I convince myself that he must have some reasoning for tormenting me the way he does. But then realization sinks in. He's just a bad person.

Edging on 280 pounds, I am obese. So much for inheriting my mother's slim figure. The apple doesn't fall far from the tree? Seems like a web of lies to me.

Somehow, my brother is the most praised boy in school—athletic, clever and nice—who doesn't like him? I was unfortunately not blessed with such good genes.

Unlike your typical high school drama, the popular kids at this school don't mix well. My brother forms his own clique and everyone wants to be them or be with them. On the flip side of the coin is Lucas' posse who seem to think that beauty is the only way to a successful life.

I fall into neither clique. I fall into you're-a-loser-and-Lucas-Keith-hates-you-so-if-I'm-nice-to-you-he-will-hate-me group. It's a sad life.

Fortunately, I have one thing going for me—my brains.

When Lucas works at McDonald's and finally realizes what it's like to be fat, I'd be working as a scientist finding a cure for cancer or being the best friend of some royalty. That would serve him right. Ha!

But at the moment, he's at the top of the food chain and I'm right at the bottom. He's the predator and I'm the prey. Brilliant. If I just hold on one more year, I'll be out of this hell hole and into real life where people don't treat fat girls like animals, a life where your weight doesn't matter. A life where the size you are in doesn't dictate the magnitude of your success.

Thankfully, I only have one more day of hell until summer starts. After that, I am a senior, reigning above the squirmy, acne-covered freshmen. But who am I kidding? I will still be below the freshmen, especially in Lucas Keith's eyes.

The books I dropped lay scattered on the floor, looking up at me in misery. *Grow a pair of balls!* They scream at me. I woefully shake my head and tell them that once again, Lucas Keith has won this battle. I slowly pick up the books and realize that I'm late for my class. Cursing under my breath, I run as fast as my legs can take me towards the door.

Heads turn one by one as I make my entrance. Sniggers to the right. Whispers to my left. I block them out and head to the last seat available. I close my eyes and sigh, falling into my seat.

"Great. Now, I can't see the board," says a low voice behind me, followed by a couple of sniggers from his faithful posse.

I turn around to see the smirking face of my bully. In an attempt to take the high road, I ignore his comment, unpack my stuff, scribble down the task Mrs. Fatimiah wrote for us on the board, and immediately start.

"Mrs. Fatto!" Lucas shouts out, using the nickname he created for our fattest teacher in the school.

"My name is Mrs. Fatimiah, Lucas. Do you have a question about the task?" She sighs, sitting on the edge of her desk. More sniggers come from the corner as the desk creaks. Her cheeks blush and I can't help but feel for her. She stands up again.

"I think something may be obstructing my view. I can't see the task." He whines. I ignore him once more. I won't let him get to me. "Oh wow! It's a person! Sorry Grace, I didn't know you were so big that you could cover the whole board."

"Lucas, we've spoken about this. Verbal abuse in the classroom gets reported to the principal," she says, trying to hold her ground. Lucas just laughs.

"I'm not scared of him. He is my uncle after all." Lucas points out, using the my-uncle-is-the-principal-so-if-you-lay-a-finger-on-me-I-will-get-you-fired card once again. Mrs. Fatimiah sighs at a loss.

"Lucas, if you really can't see, then move seats." She proposes. *Really, ma'am?* I want to ask her. *Is that really the only solution you can come up with?*

"There's no other seat in the classroom. Why don't I swap seats with you, Grace?" he asks. *Best not to get on his bad side.* I think to myself as I pull myself out of the chair. I gather up my stuff before exchanging seats wordlessly.

"Wow, this seat is warm. Also, bigger than the other one. What did you do, stretch it?" Lucas teases. I restrain from snapping back. *No, wood can't stretch you dumbass!* But again, I take the high road and ignore him for the hundredth time today.

Crack.

I suddenly hear from the small chair underneath me.

Before I know it, I'm lying sprawled on the ground, breaking the small wooden chair.

The realization hits me like a tidal wave. I broke the chair. Embarrassment overwhelms me and I feel my face heat up. Why couldn't I just last one more day? That's all it is, one day.

I'm a stranded whale on the shore—hopeless, huge, and unable to get up or get away from the public eye. My arms and legs flap around and I try to roll over. But I am hopeless. I am stuck.

Laughter roars around me, especially from a certain Lucas Keith. I thought I couldn't redden any more than I already have, but I feel another surge of heat hit my face.

I am completely and utterly stuck.

"Need a little help?" says a low voice. I look up to see Lucas hovering above me. I give him a puzzled expression. Why is he offering to help?

"Yes!" I exclaim. Lucas bends down before jerking straight back up, glory etched all over that arrogant face of his.

"I'm sorry Grace, there is no way I can lift you up. You are probably three times my weight." He laughs and his posse joins in. I should have known.

"Don't apologize," I hiss sarcastically. "I'm fine getting up by myself." I roll around some more before giving up.

"She looks like a beached whale!"

"She's so fat. You can barely see her face!"

Comments soar around me and Lucas looks much too pleased with himself. I close my eyes and before I know it, tears form around them. I can't help it as they quietly fall down. With one surge of power, I roll over and pull myself up.

"Being attractive and having every girl beg on their knees for your attention don't mean you can treat me like a piece of dirt. I happen to be the only girl in this school who hates your guts and I'm proud of it. You can make fun of my weight but at the end of the day, you'll be the one with the guilty conscience and I'll be the one who ends up with an actual life. So, screw you, Lucas!" I scream in his face before storming out of the room.

I'm done with this.

*   *   *

I wipe the tears off my face with the back of my hand and jog down the corridor, heading outside. The air is cool and I take a deep breath in to calm myself down.

I unfortunately see my brother, Will, coming through the doors with his friends. He instantly recognizes me and hurries over with a worried expression on his face.

"Grace! What happened?" he says, taking my fat face in his hands. I try to push him off me but his grip remains firm.

"Nothing!" I shout and push his muscly arms off me and carry on jogging into the car park. He is a lot fitter than me so he catches up in an instant.

"Was it Lucas again?" he asks. I shake my head. The last thing I want is for my brother to get involved. It'll only make Lucas realize his power over me.

"It's nothing. I feel ill so I'm going home," I mumble, finally reaching my car.

"Do you want me to drive you home?" he asks sincerely. I shake my head, before carefully climbing into the car.

"I'm fine. See you later Will," I tell him, before starting the engine and driving away. I allow a tear down my cheek as my surroundings rush past me. How can Lucas treat me that way? There are plenty of other overweight students at Jistie High. Why me?

I park my car in my driveway and look up at our beautiful family home. Thank goodness. Wandering into the warmth of the house, I place my jacket on the coat rack.

"Mom?" I call out, hoping she isn't home. Nobody answers and I settle myself down into the kitchen. I need some comfort

5

food. Reaching to the cupboard I retrieve a full tube of Oreos. *Twist, lick, dunk.* I think to myself after pouring a cup of milk. Why does Lucas have to be so horrible? I may be fat but I can't help it. My eyes look down to the Oreos in my hand. *Yes, you can.*

No, I can't! I reply to the small voice in my head. I was born with more meat on my bones than most girls. Even if I stopped eating all together, I would be fat still.

No, you wouldn't. You were born with your mother's figure but you ruined it.

I hit the side of my head with the tube of Oreos. *Gah!* Stupid voices. I stick my hand down the tube and take another Oreo out.

I suddenly stop, my mouth watering and my hand hovering by my open lips.

Do you really need to?

Once you've eaten that, it'll go to your stomach and make you fatter than you already are.

Why would you do that to yourself?

You're already fat.

Instead of casting the voices in my head away, I let them win the battle and place the cookie back into the tube.

That's it. You've realized, haven't you? It's your fault Lucas bullies you. You don't have to be fat.

"No, I don't."

TWO

"Hey Grace, are you here?" Will cries out when he returns from school. He gives me a bright grin, his cheeks red from soccer practice I presume.

"Yeah, I'm in the kitchen," I say, licking my fingers. I turn the blender on and it immediately starts spinning the contents of my drink around its body. Then the lid shoots off. I scream as the contents of my smoothie, if I can even call it that, splash all over the kitchen.

Will looks at me in shock. "Grace, what are you doing?"

"I'm attempting to make a smoothie," I reply feebly. "But I have no idea how to work this machine."

"God Grace, Mom is gonna freak out!" He tells me with wide eyes while running his hands through his hair. "And since when do you like tomato juice?" He picks up the carton of tomato juice and eyes it.

I shrug. "I love tomato juice. Mmm," I say, rubbing my belly. He raises an eyebrow and looks at the rest of the ingredients laid out on the table.

"Why did you mix tomato juice and milk?" He fake gags and laughs at me. "Smoothies tend to have fruit in them."

"I don't know. Milk is good for your bones, right? And tomato is a fruit according to the world wide web," I say, beginning to feel stupid.

7

"What are you doing, Grace?" he asks, cocking his head to one side. God. Having an overprotective brother really has its pitfalls.

I throw my arms up in the air. "What are you, an inspector?"

"No, but last night, I vividly remember you deciding to make yourself a pastry instead of avocado salad because you said, and I quote, '*Hate avocado so much I'd rather eat raw chicken.*'" He then folds his arms and takes a seat next to me.

I am stumped. Yes, I do remember saying that. "Alright, alright. I want to eat healthier. I whanf to loophse weyht," I mumble, some of the 'smoothie' still in my mouth.

"What?"

"I whanf to loophse weyht," I mumble again, twirling a piece of my hair around my chubby finger.

"Grace, I can't understand what you're saying." Will sighs impatiently. I shrug and try to leave the room, but a tight grip on my sleeve stops me.

"Grace . . . tell me."

"I want to lose weight, okay?! I hate having people laugh at my weight. I don't want to be laughed at for my last year of school. I don't want to cry after school most days and I definitely do not want to have to leave school because Lucas Keith bullies me to no end!" I burst out.

Will looks at me in bewilderment. "So, he's the one who made you cry. I am going to kill that . . ."

"Will! That's not the point!" I grab a sponge and begin to mop up the mess. I'm too embarrassed to see his face.

"But Grace, you're beautiful the way you are," he says kindly. I throw my arms up in frustration.

"No, I'm not! Will, what you don't realize is that I have no friends because no one wants to get on the bad side of Lucas." And it's true, I can't remember the last time I had a friend. And last time

I checked, doing someone's math homework is not the equivalent of friendship.

"My friends like you!" he shouts.

"Only because they have to or you'd make their life a living hell." Will opens his mouth to speak.

"Don't protest. You know you would."

"Okay, okay. And how exactly are you planning to lose weight?" He raises his eyebrows at the remains of my botched drink.

"Eat healthier, exercise more," I say, folding my arms. Sounds easy enough.

"You have no idea what you're doing, Grace. You can't mix tomato juice and milk." He shakes his head. I groan.

"What am I supposed to do then? I don't know good diet foods!"

"Did you not think that you could maybe look up diet plans?" he asks me, a smirk drawn on his face. I try to keep a grumpy face but soon I might have to join in with his laughter. "Look Grace, I can understand that you want to lose weight, but you need to be careful about this. Don't go overboard. Diets can end badly."

"Okay, Will."

*   *   *

I type furiously on my laptop and search.

Diet plans

Lots of things come up. I click on the first one and scan my eyes over the entire document.

The Ketogenic diet

The Ketogenic diet involves the reduction of carbohydrates in the daily diet. It works when the body ends up in ketosis, which is a stage where fat

9

storage is used as energy. This diet is useful for people who want to lose weight quickly. Common breakfasts for this diet involve eggs of any kind. Soups high in protein are popular for lunch. Dinner should be high in protein; meat or fish accompanied by a large portion of vegetables.

Sighing, I print it off and stick it on my wall. If you're going to go for it, you've got to go full out.

THREE

As I search the contact number for my local gym, I realize that I don't just want to lose weight to stop being bullied. I also want revenge. I want Lucas to feel the way I felt. He deserves it. So, step one of my revenge plan? Get a kick-ass body and show Lucas that he was wrong to treat me that way. Then, when he's begging on his knees for my attention—he's always been a sucker for sporty girls—I'll humiliate him.

But I'm getting ahead of myself. Before I can even consider how I'm going to get revenge on Lucas, I need to actually get this kick-ass body.

I dial the number for the gym, feeling my stomach in knots. I'm really doing this. *Ring ring.*

"Good afternoon, Pinewood gym, this is Amber speaking. How can I help you?" says the chirpy voice of the receptionist.

"Hi there. Um. How much is a summer membership for this gym?" I ask, fiddling with my finger nails.

"It's forty dollars a month. You can pay monthly, if you'd like. Most of our customers pay using this plan."

"Okay. I'll do that," I tell her. "So my membership will start when I do my first session, right? Can I come tomorrow?"

"Yes, of course," she says. "Do you have any more questions?"

"No, thank you very much. Bye." I end the call and let out a sigh of relief.

I put the phone down and joyfully rush downstairs. I hear voices in the kitchen, so I go and have a look. It can't be Mom because she's still at work. Obviously not dad, since he's still in Australia for his business trip unless he came home six weeks early. But I woefully doubt it.

I peer in the room. Brilliant. Will and his group of friends. The floorboards suddenly squeak underneath me, causing all four heads to turn and look my way.

I offer them a small smile and they nervously wave at me. Will beckons for me to come in.

"Oh no, it's fine. I was just seeing—"

"No, don't be silly, come and join us," Will says, chuckling. I feel myself blush and begin to wish Will wasn't such a kind older brother.

"Um," I mumble and give in to Will's pleading eyes and take a seat next to him on the sofa. His friends beam at me.

"So, Grace, Will was telling us how you're getting into fitness," Ollie asks me. I feel myself blush once more and remind myself to kill Will later.

"Yeah. I mean I'm going to try," I tell him, fumbling on my words. Ollie nods enthusiastically. I know he's a fitness enthusiast, which is part of the reason why I find it so humiliating.

"If you want, I can give you some workout plans. I know it's a whole new world which I found hard at first. I'd be more than happy to set you up," he tells me, and I see Will nod his head in approval. A small smile makes its way onto my face.

He's right. I am terrified of going to the gym and I need help. "That would be amazing. Thank you."

*   *   *

"Hi, I'm Grace Connely. I called about the monthly membership yesterday," I nervously tell the receptionist at the gym. I vaguely recognize her from school. Maybe she's in Will's grade?

12

She looks at me from head to toe, the corners of her mouth tilting up.

"Grace Connely, huh? You go to my school, Jistie High?"

I nod, embarrassed that she knows who I am. I try to lay low as much as I can and apparently it isn't working.

"Forgive my forwardness, but you're Lucas Keith's play toy, aren't you?" she asks, loudly chewing her pink gum. Thanks for pointing that out.

"Yes," I say curtly. She laughs, and I feel my face redden. Damn cheeks!

"Don't worry. He hates me too," she explains. My jaw drops. I look at her from top to bottom. She's blonde, in good shape, and totally his type.

"I know. That's what most people think," she says in response to my reaction. I feel my face redden once again. I shouldn't judge a book by its cover.

"We went out for a while. I'm sure you remember 'Lucas Keith and Amber Sevans.'" She indicates quotation marks with her fingers. She then proceeds to put her finger in her mouth indicating fake sickness. I giggle.

She's Amber Sevans? I think to myself in shock. She used to have dark hair and went out with Lucas for two years. Something happened over the summer and I assumed she left the school. I didn't even think that she had undergone a transformation.

"One summer, he wanted to take our relationship to the next level, but I said no. He then broke up with me. I left school for a year, dyed my hair blonde, and returned seemingly unrecognizable. I was able to blend in, just like that." She twirls a piece of blonde hair around her finger. "I take it you're trying to do the same thing? Blend in?"

"Kind of." I hesitate. "I want to get revenge on him. He's made my life a living hell. It's his turn."

"Honey, it isn't that easy. Trust me, I tried," she tells me.

"I'll try harder.'"

13

"Then the only thing I have to say to you is good luck. You'll need it. He's a hard shell to crack."

I nod and head over to the treadmill, Ollie's workout plan in hand. Let's get down to business.

*   *   *

After half an hour, I'm already covered in sweat and unable to go on. How do people manage to do this every day?

I decide to take a break from the treadmill and go on the cycling machine to work my legs. Ollie told me that starting off with cardio should help increase my stamina and then I can move onto strength

Before I climb on, I take a sip of the energy drink I bought from the protein section in the store. It gives me the shivers and makes me gag every time but at least it gives me the strength to continue.

I haul my leg over the cycling seat and turn the resistance up to five. I then start pedaling, immediately feeling an ache running down my leg but I manage to power through. With the little strength I have left, I climb off the bike. I grab the energy drink and gulp as much as I can. I close my eyes out of exhaustion and take a 5-minute break. Then I head to the weights, take the lightest one, and begin to work my arms.

After a while, my arms are too sore to carry on, so I decide to do some crunches instead. After working my abs on the mats for the final stretch, I leave the gym. I collapse in my car, hungry and tired.

I drive home as quickly as I can, eager to make myself some lunch. When I enter the living room, I see my brother and his friends hanging out. I guess they stayed the night and weren't up when I left this morning.

I smile nervously and watch them as they eye my tracksuit and baggy t-shirt, both covered in a disgusting amount of sweat.

I feel myself redden and run into the kitchen to cook myself a cup of soup. I look in the fridge and find myself a low-calorie chicken soup. *Low calorie. I bet that won't fill me up.* My stomach growls sadly as I take the packet out of the fridge and pour it into a saucepan.

I check my phone as I let the soup warm up. No messages. What a surprise, as if I expect to see otherwise.

When the soup boils, I carefully pour it into a bowl and drink it as quickly as I can without burning my tongue and throat. My stomach growls unhappily again. I pat it gently, making the rolls wobble. "I'm sorry, but this is the only way I can get rid of you," I tell it as if it's a real person, before wolfing down the rest of the soup. After my lunch, if I can call it that, I go upstairs to see if I have magically lost some weight.

Nope, still 280 pounds. Sighing, I mentally curse myself for being so naïve for thinking that I would lose weight that quickly.

Forgetting my childish ways, I grab my laptop and roam Netflix for a new TV series to binge watch. No judgment please, that's what summer is for, right?

Before I know it, it's 9 p.m. and I feel my eyes beginning to shut. My body is definitely not used to being under this amount of strain. But as I feel myself drift off and my muscles begin to ache, I feel a sense of satisfaction.

I'm actually doing this.

FOUR

I wake up with sore legs. I can barely move as I swing my legs out of my bed and attempt to get up. I groan and shuffle down the stairs. I can barely carry my own weight.

"Grace?" says Mom. "Do you want a fried breakfast?"

I think about it for a moment. Imagine the satisfaction . . . the taste on my tongue . . .

"No thanks, Mom. I'll have eggs."

"Eggs? Do you want some bacon?" she asks, her voice hinting with worry. I shrug as I enter the kitchen to give her a good morning hug.

"No thanks," I mumble, while my inner voice screams *yes*. I gulp and look down at my pathetic-sized breakfast. My stomach grumbles quietly before I take a mouthful of my plain eggs. Who said I even liked eggs?

After breakfast, I head down to the gym for another session, even though my legs can barely move. I look down at my feet as I walk, a habit I picked up from my days at school—head down, eyes down and hoping not to get into any trouble. Not that it worked 100%.

"If it isn't big fat Grace Connely," says a snide voice. I feel my pulse quicken and my hands grow damp. Before I can stop it, a little whimper escapes from my mouth. I bring my hand up to my mouth immediately to mask it, but he's already heard it.

16

"Is someone a bit scared? You know, you got me into a lot of trouble. I don't like it when someone crosses my path like that." His head tilts to one side. "Especially not a fat little cow like you."

I find some courage deep, deep down and muster up a response. "I don't like it when someone comments on my weight. I guess we don't all get what we want, do we?" I reply, raising my eyebrows. He looks shocked. I am shocked by my bravery myself.

"Don't be sarcastic with me, Grace, or I'll get angry," he says through gritted teeth and I see him clench his fists.

"Oh, I have a name now?" I chuckle. "Look, you're not my father. You can't tell me what to—" I get cut off when suddenly a harsh slap hits my face. It stings so much that tears form in my eyes almost immediately. He sees the tears in my eyes and smirks triumphantly.

"Get away from me, fat cow. I don't want to ever see you—"

A punch is thrown at his face but it's not from me. I don't have the muscle power to do that yet. That's still a work in progress.

I turn around to see who has come to save the day and be my knight in shining armor. Slicked back black hair and tight jeans. He looks like he's just stepped out of *Grease*. Danny Zuko, is that you?

"Are you okay? Jeez. I can't believe he just hit you," he asks, touching my arm. The pain fizzles in my cheek as confusion runs through my mind.

"I'll be fine. Thank you for stopping him." I smile. "But who are you?" I ask him. He chuckles and shrugs.

"Jacob Sanders. And you're Grace, right?" he says. I quickly wipe away a tear that had been rolling down my face before smiling a little. *He knows me?* It appears my attempt at staying off the grid was a complete failure. Good job, Grace!

"Do you live here?" I ask him. He shrugs.

"Yeah, hun." He shakes his fist. "Wow that really hurt my hand." He turns his attention back to Lucas.

"First of all, why are you bullying a poor girl?" he yells. Lucas wipes his face and looks at Jacob with eyes full of hatred. "And second, I'm bringing a boxing glove next time. My hands are too sensitive to punch," he says confidently. I withhold a giggle.

"Who do you think you are?" Lucas shouts, pushing Jacob backwards with force. Jacob's eyes narrow and he returns the shove harder.

"You are going to ruin my Gucci jacket!" he tells him before shaking his head. "But that's beside the point. You need to leave her alone. She has done nothing to you. Why do you feel the need to bully her huh?" Jacob says firmly, anger biting at his words.

"She's fat. Fat people annoy me, therefore, she annoys me. It's not rocket science." Lucas smirks. Jacob throws another punch, breaking his promise of wearing gloves the next time but Lucas catches his fist. I see Lucas begin to squeeze Jacob's fist, making Jacob shout in pain.

So, I do what any girl would do in that situation. I kick him where it hurts.

*　　*　　*

Lucas is now lying on the ground, screaming in agony, while Jacob films it. I would have never thought he'd be a good fighter. I then slowly recognize his face from school. He's slightly skinnier than most of the boys at our school and a lot smaller. But that didn't seem to stop him from practically beating Lucas up, despite his claim of having 'sensitive hands'.

"Jacob, thank you so much. That was seriously awesome. I owe you." I grin. He shrugs and winks at me.

"It's no big deal. I've always wanted to have an excuse to kick his ass." He places his arm on my shoulder. "It's lovely to meet you properly, Grace."

18

I bite my lip. "You too. I gotta go though, the gym is calling," I tell him and he nods.

"Yeah, of course. See you."

"Bye." I say, but he quickly grabs my arm.

"Don't let him bully you into getting skinnier," he gently says. I shrug.

"It's not that simple."

*   *   *

After my gym session, my legs ache more than they've ever done before, making me walk awkwardly.

I walk into the kitchen slowly, seeing Mom cooking in the kitchen. The sweet aroma fills my nose and I sigh with pleasure. Dammit, why does she have to be such a good cook?

"Any lunch for you, honey bun?" She pushes a strand of her golden blonde hair behind her ear then smooth's down her white working dress. I sigh in jealousy and awe at the same time. Fashionable. Skinny. Pretty. Cooler than me. She's everything I'm not.

"No thanks. I'm having soup," I tell her and she sighs. Here it comes.

"Honey, don't go overboard with this—"

I cut her off. "That's what Will said. I'm the last person in the world that would go anorexic. Look at me." I gesture to my stomach. "You need to realize that I probably won't even end up losing weight. Just let me try and at the least fail with dignity?"

"Fine, but please don't go overboard," she says sympathetically.

"I know Mom, I know." I shrug and begin to walk up the stairs.

"Grace, I thought you were having soup?" she asks. I shake my head.

19

"I'm not that hungry. I'll have it for supper instead," I tell her, and she nods. She says something under her breath and I immediately know it's about me but I leave it. She doesn't know what it's like.

FIVE

Ding dong!

I wake up suddenly from my peaceful slumber and quickly get out of bed. To my great despair, Mom has gone to Paris for fashion week and my brother has soccer practice so I am alone at home.

Unfortunately, my reactions are a little slower than usual, therefore, causing me to fall over with a large impact. I make an inhumane sound before getting up and pulling my hoodie over my pink pajamas. The doorbell rings again and I groan.

"I'm coming!" I trudge down the stairs slowly. It's probably Will. Maybe soccer practice was cancelled and he lost his keys. It won't be anyone coming to see me.

I slowly open the door. To my surprise, I see Jacob in his usual Danny Zuko getup. I raise an eyebrow at him. Am I dreaming?

"What?" is the only word I say. Especially at this time of the morning.

"Morning," he says chirpily, looking through into my house. I narrow my eyes in confusion.

"How—" I begin, but Jacob cuts me off.

"I asked around, okay. I'm not a psycho, and I just wanted to come and say hi." He chuckles. "So, hi."

"Erm hi," I say uncertainly. "Jacob, it's 8 o'clock in the morning."

"Yeah," he says, picking his nails, completely unfazed by the time of day.

"Why the hell did you wake me up?" I ask, slightly angry. He chuckles, and I realize I've been harsh. I take a breath and step backwards. "Sorry. Please do come in. Would you like some breakfast?" I lead him into the kitchen.

"Sure. What are we having?" He sits himself down at the table. *Sure. Make yourself at home.* But my rational side is reminding me that he came over to see me. Me. Does this mean I finally have a friend?

"Scrambled eggs." He looks disappointed. "I'm on a diet, sorry."

He frowns. "I know what you're trying to do." His mouth turns into a smirk. I raise my eyebrows.

"Oh, do you now?" I fold my arms and stare at this 'almost' stranger across my kitchen. He smirks and runs his hand through his slicked back hair.

"You're trying to lose weight to get back at Lucas." He pauses to look at me. "Am I right?"

"That was a good guess. I'll give you that." I crack the eggs into a cup and whisk them. He chuckles.

"What can I say? I'm good at reading people." He shrugs. "I can help you out if you'd like. I have a friend who does miracles on hair because honey, your hair needs to be fixed." My mouth drops open, slightly taken aback by his blunt delivery.

"Why on earth do you want to help me?" I ask him with a frown on my face. We've been at the same school for years and only now he wants to become friends with me. It all sounds a little suspicious.

"I have a lot of friends that have been treated badly by Lucas, myself included." His tone becomes more serious. "So, I know how it feels. I think it's time he learns his lesson." My frown lessens and I smile, because for the first time at Jistie, I feel like I have met someone who understands what I've been through.

22

"So, are you up for it?" Jacob gives me a grin and I nod. He has become way too invested in my plan.

"You're going to march up to him and introduce yourself as—"

I cut Jacob off. "No. I'm not using a fake identity. This isn't a movie, Jacob." I roll my eyes. He's so dramatic.

"But—" He looks put out.

"Trust me. It would just go wrong."

"Fine. But that means you've got to look hotter than I originally planned . . ." He mumbles for a couple of seconds before snapping his fingers. "You need a new wardrobe."

"I thought so. My clothes only consist of sweatpants and grey t-shirts. Mom is in Paris at the moment, I guess she could pick out some things?" I tell Jacob and he delightedly claps his hands.

"Perfect! Gucci has an incredible summer line out," he tells me. And then I realize I have no idea what size I'll be when this is finished. I don't want my mom to be spending unnecessary money, not that she needs to worry about her expenditure, when I might not even manage this.

"What if I don't manage it?" I ask, my emotions dampened. "What if I never actually lose weight?"

"You will. I'm going to make sure you're a six," Jacob tells me.

My mouth falls open. "No way. I won't be a six in a million years."

"If you put your mind into it, honey, you could be a four by Christmas," he tells me with a knowing look. I blink once. Twice. Three times.

"Are you crazy?" I fire back. He chuckles at my reaction and grabs an apple from the fruit bowl.

"A little crazy is good, peaches." He pinches my cheeks, so I swat him away.

"Fine, I'll give her a call." I grab my phone and dial Mom's number.

"Hello?" says Mom, already with a hint of French accent like it always does when she goes to France.

"Hey Mom, it's me," I say. Jacob wiggles his shoulders sassily and clicks his fingers. That boy is the definition of extra.

"Hey darling. You okay home alone?"

"Yeah. I was just wondering since you're in Paris, maybe you could pick me up some clothes like Gucci or something?" The words seem foreign in my mouth.

"Since when do you like designer clothes?"

"Since I want to be a size six," I tell her. The line goes silent for a minute.

"Grace, remember what I said the other day," she tells me sternly, and I take a deep breath. Why can't my family just support me? Surely, they'd want me to be healthy?

"Can you get the clothes or not?" I ask, before adding 'please' to make it less demanding.

"Okay darling. Okay." She hangs up abruptly. I give Jacob a big grin.

"Green light!" I tell him enthusiastically. He beams in return.

"So, we're sorted. You're going to look fab." He clicks his fingers once more.

"We've known each other for what, two days or less. And you—" He cuts me off.

"Time is just a number." Jacob raises his eyebrows at me. I roll my eyes.

"Wrong context, honey."

SIX

Three weeks later

Beep beep beep beep

Blurts my alarm. I groan and roll over to turn the irritating noise off. My eyes widen when I see the time.

10 o'clock?! I forgot to set my alarm earlier on!

I jump out of bed and throw my now slightly baggy sweatpants and t-shirt before running downstairs and out of the door. Breakfast will have to wait until I get home. A little hungry, I reach the gym a couple of minutes late.

"Hey Amber, so sorry I'm late!" I tell her.

"Chillax girl, you're not at school," she drawls. Over the past month, Amber and I have become a lot closer which is unsurprising since I see her every day. She's also coincidentally best friends with Jacob. Apparently, their parents go way back.

I head straight over to the cycling machine since I forgot to go on it yesterday.

My legs are still extremely sore so I wince as I throw my leg over the seat. I immediately start pedaling and build sweat almost instantly.

By the end of the session, my stomach is growling so loudly that I'm now receiving weird looks from the other people around me. I feebly smile at them, telling them I didn't have any breakfast.

"Jeez, woman, you're like a machine," Amber tells me with laughter in her eyes. I shrug before my stomach lets out an almighty roar.

"A machine which is going to concave without any food." I laugh and she laughs with me, before running out of the gym to my car.

I rush home and cook myself some scrambled eggs. I shove them onto a plate and take it upstairs with me to watch the Vampire Diaries. I collapse on my bed and shovel the eggs into my mouth so quickly that my stomach begins to ache from indigestion.

After watching a couple of episodes on Netflix, I realize it's been a month since I last started working out. I must have lost weight by now—my clothes are getting baggy. So, I decide to take a leap of faith and weigh myself. I near the scales. Surprisingly, my stomach bursts into little butterflies. I take a breath. This is the moment of truth whether my hard-core diet and workouts have paid off. I take a small step and stand on the scales. I breathe in and look down. My jaw drops. That can't be right . . .

I have lost forty-two pounds. Two hundred and twenty pounds! Eighty pounds away from my target!

I jump in glee and look down at my body to inspect it—a couple of rolls on my stomach and my thighs still touch at the top but there is significant change.

Pride fills my heart. It worked! I can't believe it actually worked. Life has immediately brightened. Also, Dad is coming back in two weeks and I go back to school in seven weeks where I will have hopefully reached my target.

I run downstairs as quickly as I can to see my brother in the kitchen with Ollie.

Ollie looks at me with confusion. "Grace? Is that you?"

"She's showing some progress, isn't she, Ollie? Remember when you gave her your workouts? Clearly they worked a charm."

"Wow, you've lost a ton of weight," he compliments, looking me up and down. Still, I'm obviously not as skinny as most girls in our school, far from it. Plus, my hair is still a frizzy wreck and my dress sense sucks. But I guess when I can fit into the amazing clothes from Paris, I'll be fine and on trend. Hopefully it will all work out as planned.

"Thanks. And Will, that's what I came downstairs to tell you! Guess how much weight I've lost?" I ask him, my smile broadening.

"I dunno . . . ten pounds?" he questions.

"No, silly, forty-two!" I say gleefully. His jaw drops, before his expression turns to be extremely worried.

"Grace, that's quite unhealthy. How much more do you plan to lose?" he asks, raking his hands through his hair.

"About eighty pounds. I want to be 140 pounds and then I'll be happy," I tell him. He shakes his head.

"No, Grace, stop eating so little and stop going to the gym," he demands. "I don't think that much weight loss is healthy."

I frown and I want to scream at him. "You have no idea what it was like. I want to have a good last year, not one where I am known as the girl who tried to lose weight and failed." I pause. "I don't care what you say Will. I'm going to lose this last bit of weight if it is the last thing I do."

SEVEN

Ding dong

"Get the door, Will!" I yell from my room. I hear him groan from his and he shuffle down the stairs.

Ding dong

"I'm coming!" he moans, and I hear the door open followed by several voices.

"Grace, it's for you!" I hear him yell. I climb out of bed, wondering who it is. It can't be Jacob as he's on holiday in Peru (lucky boy). I rush downstairs, eager to find out who would bother driving to my house to see me of all people.

I try to see past Will to see who it is without any luck. Will is chatting lively to her (I can see that much) and keeps on scuffing up his hair. I frown in confusion. Will only plays with his hair when he's nervous. And Will hardly ever gets nervous.

As I approach the door, I finally see who it is. Blonde hair, tanned skin, and pink bubblegum. Amber?

"Hey Grace," says her chirpy voice and then Will finally lets her into the house. She's laughing a little at my shocked expression while Will burns bright red. I give him a look but he avoids my eye contact, how weird.

"Hey Amber." Amber and I definitely are friends, I do see her every day. Plus, she's besties with Jacob. I just didn't think we were good enough friends for her to come over. I guess I was wrong.

"Can we talk?" she asks, her blonde hair bouncing on her small shoulders. I nod and beckon her further inside. Will follows us into the kitchen like a lost puppy. He's clearly never seen someone as attractive as Amber and I don't disagree with him. She's gorgeous.

"So, I was on the phone with Jacob the other day and he mentioned that he's helping you with your revenge plan. Can I be part of the team too?" she blurts out, causing my mouth to drop open. She laughs at my reaction before continuing.

"I want to get revenge on Lucas too. He broke my heart," she says, pretending to wipe a tear from below her eye. "Just kidding, I couldn't have cared less about him, but he ruined me. So, I wanna ruin him too." She shrugs and both Will and I have the same expression on our faces.

What the . . .

"Well. Erm. I'll leave you, erm, girls to it?" Will says, clearly unsure of what to say. Amber laughs gracefully, being perfect like she is, which makes Will redden further and then he scuttles away into the kitchen.

"Yeah, I mean . . . sure thing." The words fumble out of my mouth. Amber gives me a bright grin.

"So, what does this revenge plan entail then?" She sits down on a stool and places her head on her hands, full attention on me.

"I haven't really thought about it, to be honest. I just figured that if I could get a good body then I could show him that he was wrong to bully me all those years." I shrug. Amber claps her hands together joyfully.

"I think that's an awesome idea." Then she launches into several ideas that she has about this revenge plan, making my mind whirl. She and Jacob have definitely given this more thought than I have.

"Anyway, those ideas are just off the top of my head. We can think about it more before school starts," she says with a grin.

Thankfully, her phone begins to ring, meaning she won't continue to lecture me about the revenge plan. It's making me feel nervous. I zone out while Amber speaks on the phone, my stomach spinning at the idea of returning to school to see Lucas.

"Okay, Pete, thanks. I'll see you later." Amber hangs up the phone with a devilish look on her face. "So, what do you want to do, Grace? Want to come to a party with me?"

*   *   *

After a lot of convincing, Amber finally manages to persuade me to go to a party with her but I did not go down without a fight. I was mainly confused as to why she wanted me, of all people, to go with her to a party. She claims that she'd wanted to invite me to a load of parties before but Jacob told her that I wouldn't want to. He was right, I guess.

She's dressed me head to toe in her largest clothes. The dress is tight around my stomach but other than that it fits fine. It's a size 10 and I am happy. To think that she was once a size 10 is hard to believe—she told me it was after the break up. Apparently, she ate loads and realized how much it affected her so she started working at the gym which meant a free gym membership.

She has me in a tight green dress but I insist on wearing my favorite denim jacket so it covers up where my fat shows. She then tries to apply her perfected makeup skills on my plain face but I beg her to stop, so she only applies a little mascara. I am still plain old Grace Connely.

Now we sit in her car, waiting to go into the loud party. She says that she only has friends who don't go to Jistie High (except for Jacob), and that this party is for Cranbrook High students. I understand her reasoning because the people at Jistie suck. I like to think that's why I don't have any friends there, but realistically I know the real reason. Lucas Keith.

"Come on Grace, we've got to go in!" Amber demands, while pulling my arm with great strength. I don't budge.

"I can't believe I missed my gym session for this," I grumble. Recently, I've been feeling guilty when I don't go to the gym. It's a good feeling. It motivates me.

"You're crazy. You're the first person I've met who actually would rather be working out than be at a party."

"Either way, I will be surrounded by sweaty people." I laugh, attempting to make a joke to calm my nerves. Amber doesn't find it quite so funny.

"Come on, Grace! I don't get why you're so nervous." She tugs at my arm again but I shake my head.

"I've never been to a party before." I say, my voice shaking slightly. To be honest, I don't know why I'm so nervous.

"Come on, Grace. When we go back to school, you're gonna be invited to tons of parties. Just get this over and done with and you'll know what a party is like." She tugs my arm once more, so I finally give in and climb slowly out of the car. I pull my dress down slightly. Amber runs around me and grabs my hand, pulling me quickly towards the house with music booming out of it.

As we enter the party, a wave of heat hits me, alongside the smell of vodka, smoke, and weed. Amber greets a few people, while also being wolf-whistled several times. I just receive looks of confusion. I pull my jacket around me tighter. I shouldn't have come to this. An extremely attractive boy approaches Amber and crashes his lips to hers. She smiles into the kiss and pulls him closer. I look around at my surroundings while I wait for them to finish. Whoever's party this is has definitely got wealthy parents. The hall is huge!

When Amber and the mysterious guy finally pull away from each other, Amber's lipstick is already off her face.

"Kyle, this is my friend, Grace. Grace, this is Kyle, my boyfriend." She grins. Kyle holds his hand out to me and I take it gently.

31

"Nice to meet you," I tell him, and he smiles. Amber loops her arm around his neck before telling me she's going to get us a drink. I nod and tell her I'll wait here.

Now I know nobody. I wander over to a small sofa which is unoccupied, so I hastily sit on it and pull my dress down my legs so less flesh is shown. I tilt my head back and close my eyes, letting the music run through me. At least the DJ has good music taste.

"I'm baack!" Amber calls as she approaches my sofa with a solo cup in her hand. Her boyfriend follows her like a puppy.

"What is it?" I shout, attempting to be heard over the loud music. She winks at me and holds her cup out.

"Cheers to you, Grace!" She clinks her glass to mine before raising it to her lips and drinking the entire cup. My mouth drops open.

"That's my girl!" Kyle cheers and wolf whistles. I eye my drink suspiciously and take her lead. Screw it! The first sip is punchy, but as I manage to glug the rest, I feel it go down more smoothly. Amber whoops and Kyle gives me a clap.

"Good job!" Amber high fives me, and I feel myself buzzing. I feel more relaxed. Amber grabs my hand and takes me over to a circle of people, who appear to be playing a drinking game.

"Want to play?" Amber asks. "They're playing truth or dare."

"Um. I don't know." I bite my lip awkwardly. "I don't know anyone." The pounding music hits me hard in the head and the smell of alcohol makes me want to throw up.

"Come on Grace. It'll be fun." She hands me another drink. "Liquid courage."

"I don't know Amber . . ." I start to feel uncomfortable. She gives me a look. "I don't know anyone!"

"You already said that. My friend Pete is playing too and he's awesome. We can sit with him." She takes my hand and I decide to be brave. My weight loss has already gained me two more friends. I'd love another.

Amber guides me to the group and takes a seat in the circle. I follow her lead awkwardly and look around the circle. To my amazement, no one even spares a look at me. No one turns to see why big fat Grace Connely has come to a party. I fit in.

"Grace, this is Pete. He goes to Jistie too." Amber snaps me out of my trance. I turn my attention to her and see an absolutely gorgeous boy holding his hand out. It takes me a few moments to realize he's offering to shake my hand. How polite.

"I'm Grace." I shake his hand and try to keep my cheeks from blushing. It's hard being around such attractive guys, especially since this time a month ago he probably wouldn't have spared me a single look. Let alone a handshake.

"It's lovely to meet you, Grace." He gives me a genuine grin. I smile back at him. "Bad luck," he tells me, a mischievous look on his face. I frown in confusion.

"What?"

"The bottle has landed on you. Truth or dare?" He chuckles. I sigh and turn my attention back to the circle, where all eyes are on me. The boy who last spun the bottle raises his eyebrow at me, encouraging me to pick.

"Truth?" I tell him, unsure of what he's going to ask me. He ponders for a couple of seconds before scratching his chin.

"Who do you hate the most in this world?" he asks me, clearly aware I'm new to the game. Otherwise, I'm sure the question would have been worse. But I'm grateful and I know the answer straight away.

"Lucas Keith," I say as confidently as I can. The whole room goes quiet and I wonder if they know who he is, seeing as they go to a different school.

"What's your name?" the boy who asked me the game question asks.

33

"Grace," I say nervously. All eyes are on me and I feel as if I said something wrong. But they don't know who Lucas is, right?

"Grace," the boy says with a smirk on his face. "Welcome to Cranbrook High!" Then the room bursts into cheer. I look around to see Amber with a proud look on her face.

"They hate Lucas too. He used to go to Cranbrook but he was expelled for bullying," Amber tells me and I feel a warming sensation at the bottom of my stomach. A feeling I have never experienced before, and despite this, I know exactly what it is. A sense of belonging.

*　　*　　*

A couple more drinks in and I begin to feel drunk. Amber is, too, and Pete is barely managing to keep her upright.

"So, if you go to Jistie, what brings you here?" I ask Pete. Since meeting him, I have had constant butterflies in my stomach. I think I might have a small crush.

"Is this party not an explanation in itself?" Pete gestures to the surroundings before helping Amber down onto the sofa. An inhumane noise comes from her mouth, causing me and Pete to burst into laughter.

"Yeah. Everyone here seems really nice." I shrug. "Plus, they all hate Lucas too so that's a bonus."

"I guess." He cocks his head to the side and looks at me. "You know, Grace, I barely recognized you when Amber introduced you."

My stomach drops. So he's realized who I am. Fantastic. "Yeah. I guess the weight loss can't hide everything."

"I used to see you around school a lot. Your brother is Will, right?" he asks and I nod. "He's a good guy. I saw the way Lucas treated you, but I never did anything about it. No one did."

"It's okay. I never expected anyone to do anything. Lucas controls Jistie." I bite my lip because it's true.

"I know." He sighs. "Anyway, I think it's time Amber gets home. She's a wreck." I look at the slumped position of my new friend and chuckle.

She is a wreck indeed.

"I've got her," I tell him before hauling her up with my new muscles. "It was great to meet you, Pete."

"You too, Grace. I hope to see you around."

Hello, butterflies.

EIGHT

One month left

Jacob is back from Peru. He and Amber seem to live at my house now, not that I'm complaining. I've found two awesome friends and I love their company.

I haven't weighed myself since last month mainly because I forgot, being so busy with the gym and my new-found social life.

Jacob sits eagerly on the edge of my bed. "You go, girlfriend." He puts his fist in the air before slicking back his hair. I might start calling him Danny Zuko. I think it would suit him.

I shuffle over to the scales, taking a deep breath. I step on the scales gingerly and gulp. The moment of truth.

I hear a squeak from Jacob. Really good news or really bad news. I suspect the latter. Glancing down at my feet, I feel my stomach drop.

Fifty pounds. I've lost fifty pounds!

I stare at the numbers in disbelief. It's unreal, unheard of. I can't begin to explain the shock I'm feeling.

"That's not normal," Jacob points out. I look at him with wide eyes. No shit, Sherlock.

"Like hell." I run my hand through my hair. "The Ketogenic diet is supposed to speed up your metabolism by crazy amounts but I never expected this."

Jacob's eyes widen. "And let's be real, you have good genes. I bet you used to have a fast metabolism but unhealthy eating slowed it down. By eating less and exercising more, you've been able to lose an incredible amount of weight."

I step off the scales and wander over to my mirror. Since I didn't make a habit of looking in the mirror before I lost weight, I definitely didn't start looking in the mirror more.

I gasp when I see my reflection. I . . . actually have a figure instead of rolls of fat. I suddenly notice how my sweatpants fall on me. Loose, the same with my t-shirt. Nothing fits anymore.

Before I can help myself, a huge grin falls onto my face. 170 pounds! Only 30 pounds away from my goal! I couldn't help but wonder if I'd even be less than 140 pounds before school started.

Jacob claps his hands joyously and dances around the room. Even though he hasn't admitted it to me, I know he's gay.

And no, I'm not making assumptions. When stealing his phone before, I've seen his texts between him and this 'Javi' dude. And they were not innocent texts, let me tell you.

"I can't wait until the end of next month!" he cheers. At the end of August, he's taking me to get my hair done, an attempt to get rid of my mousy frizz which is pathetically attempting to be hair.

I look at him with a tired look. "I'm exhausted, Jacob. Can we just go to bed now?" I ask sadly.

He shakes his head. "Nope. Amber's coming around soon and then we can tell her the great news."

I groan and fall back onto my bed. I love my best friends but sometimes they are exhausting.

The doorbell rings and of course, Will answers it. He seems to have been taken aback by Amber, no matter how many times I tell him she has a boyfriend.

"Afternoon, my little chickens!" Amber announces as she enters the room. Jacob and I laugh at her weirdness. She then plops down on the bed.

"So? How much?" she asks. I open my mouth to speak but Jacob beats me to it.

"170!" Jacob blurts out before I can say anything. I hit his arm playfully. "Sorry, I know you wanted to break the news. But 170! That's insane, Grace."

"Well done!" Amber throws her arms around me. "You're awesome."

"Thanks." I grin, feeling impressed with myself. Amber looks at Jacob, mischief in her eyes. I frown in confusion.

"Should I tell her?" Amber asks and Jacob giggles like a thirteen-year-old girl. Tell me what?

"Hello?" I wave my hand in front of their faces to get their attention. "Care to enlighten me?" Amber grins and takes my hand in hers.

"I was having coffee with Pete the other day and we started talking about the party." She looks at Jacob who giggles once more. I roll my eyes, attempting to hide the butterflies in my stomach that appeared when Pete's name was mentioned.

"And?" I urge her.

"He told me he thinks you're beautiful!" She squeals and the butterflies in my stomach erupt into pterodactyls. I tilt my head to one side. Surely not. Someone as gorgeous as Pete can't find me attractive?

"Are you messing with me?" I ask her, because if she is, that's a cruel joke. She shakes her head and so does Jacob.

"He really said that. You're hot, Grace!" Amber nudges my shoulder and I can't help but grin. Step one of my revenge plan is nearly complete.

*   *   *

After Jacob and Amber leave, I decide to make a trip to the gym. Amber's confession about Pete's thoughts on me have given me motivation to make this final stretch. Then, I'll be ready to get revenge on Lucas.

I wander out of the house and jog down the road. I suddenly see a boy walking on my side of the road. As he comes closer, I recognize him. Speak of the devil and he shall appear.

No.

Oh no.

No way.

It couldn't be.

Could it?

I keep my head down, hoping to avoid a bad incident with Lucas. He seems to be in a hurry. He comes closer and I make the mistake of looking up. Our eyes meet and I feel my heart beat quicken.

But the oddest thing happens. Lucas Keith . . . the boy who's bullied me for as long as I can remember, smiles at me.

"Hey," he says as he passes me. I frown in confusion. I carry on walking until I hear his voice behind me.

"Are you new around here?" he asks casually. I turn around to look at him and he still doesn't recognize me. He's still smiling and tilts his head to the side.

"Um," I murmur, "no."

"I'm Lucas." He holds his hand out for me to shake. I glance down at it before meeting his eyes again. I put my hands into the pockets of my hoodie.

"Germaphobe. Gotta go. Bye." I turn away from my bully and pace away from him. I hear him call after me but my only response is to quicken my pace.

*　　*　　*

The gym is pretty uneventful.

39

As I take even steps on the running machine, I can't help but wonder when dad's going to get home. He's been on a business trip in Australia since the beginning of summer and I really miss him.

I imagine what it would be like to live in Australia. Imagine all those Australian boys around you. I mean, who doesn't like Australian accents? They make a person 100% better looking. Okay, maybe that's a little over the top but you get the gist.

When my session finishes, I say goodbye to Amber who looks exhausted. "As if you're working out," I tell her.

"I think my energy is in the minus numbers," she says back to me as I pass the counter.

"Well, exercise releases endorphins. Endorphins make you happy!" I wink at her, quoting my favorite film. She rolls her eyes before waving me off.

I jog home, hoping to miss any sighting of Lucas. When I walk through the front door, I hear Mom yelling at the phone.

"This is ridiculous, Rob! You've been away for the whole summer! You have two children who miss you so much and one who you probably wouldn't even recognize anymore! If they extend your stay one more time, I swear to God I will come over there and bring you back home myself!"

A faded crackle of my dad's calming voice is heard. I stay behind the door. I don't want her to know I'm here. This explains why dad didn't come back as planned. He was supposed to be back weeks ago.

"I don't care if you're helping an architecture trainee! He can learn with someone else!" she yells, her face red and blotchy. She's been crying.

My dad says something else.

"Bring him back here then! Surely, he can work on the plan with you when he's here? He can stay in the guest room, Rob. We can work around this. Come back here okay?" Her voice becomes softer.

My dad's voice is so quiet I can't even hear a murmur. Mom hangs up and puts her head in her hands. I choose this moment to come into the room.

"Hey Mom, are you okay? Were you talking to Dad?" I ask.

"I'm fine. He'll be back by the end of August. They've extended his stay again. He's working with a trainee who needs to sort out a visa to come here. Once that's sorted, he can bring the trainee back here and your father won't have to leave again."

"Here?" I ask, wondering if 'here' means the Pinewood, or my actual home.

"I think he's going to stay in the spare room, if that's okay with you and Will?" She looks hopeful, so I can't help but nod. I hate that she is so sad. But secretly, I can't think of anything worse than having some stranger living next to my room. I hide my concerns and take her hand.

"We'll see him soon. And we're ok, right? We've waited this long, haven't we?" I say weakly. I do miss him a lot.

NINE

End of August

The climax. My final weight before I go back to school. Jacob and Amber sit on the edge of my bed eagerly. I step onto the scales and look down. I gasp and so do Jacob and Amber. 130 pounds! Ten pounds lighter than my goal!

I take a look in the mirror and see a dramatic difference. No rolls anymore. Where there used to be fat, slim curves are seen. My legs no longer press together at the top. Even my face has slimmed. I can't help it. I squeal in joy! My friends join in too before leaping up to give me a hug. We dance around the room before Jacob stops us.

"Guys, you know what time it is now," Jacob says in a feminine voice. I roll my eyes. I know exactly what's crossing his mind.

"Hair!" They both shriek, jumping with joy. I face-palm and hope they won't be like this for the whole day. Oh, but how wrong was I.

Two enthusiastic hands grab mine before rushing me out of the door. With confusion etched on my face, the two fashion obsessed geeks smile sheepishly at me as we reach my front door.

I shrug my coat on and follow Jacob and Amber out of the door and down the stairs, matching in double denim. We pile into

Jacob's car which suspiciously smells of Abercrombie and Fitch, a cologne he doesn't wear.

The engine roars to life and we drive down the road to the final step in my revenge plan. After ten minutes, we reach a small cabin, something similar to a house you would find in the middle of a ski resort. Unsure of where Jacob has taken us, I remain in the car.

Jacob flashes me a cheeky grin before getting out of the car and wandering up to a tall boy who's Latino-looking, with dark hair, and stubble glittered across his perfectly defined jaw. As Jacob reaches him, they embrace and kiss.

I jolt back in surprise. This is Jacob's boyfriend? *Good job!* is my first thought because damn, that boy is attractive. When Jacob has . . . finished, he turns and gestures towards me. I redden again, before climbing out of the car and shuffling over to the couple. Amber skips around me and shakes the boy's hand. I feel it's wrong to call him a boy. He must be at least twenty.

"This is Javi," Jacob says as I approach the couple. I reach out and shake his warm hand. A whiff of Abercrombie and Fitch cologne confirms my earlier suspicions.

"I have heard much about you." Javi chuckles, his voice thick with a Mexican accent. His dark eyes glitter and I silently congratulate Jacob once more. This boy must be a Calvin Klein model.

"And I haven't heard enough about you." A small smile creeps onto my face and my eyes dart between the two boys.

"Javi is my boyfriend, Grace," Jacob states confidently. I roll my eyes.

"No way," I say sarcastically. "I've seen the texts." Jacob's face pales. I wink at Javi.

"I never told you I was gay, though," he says, his face etched with confusion. "Javi could have been a friend of mine."

"I told you, I have seen the texts." I chuckle at Jacob's expression. He looks embarrassed but Javi just chuckles and presses his lips to Jacob's forehead.

"I'm putting a passcode on my phone, you sneaky little devil." He nudges my shoulder before laughing. "Anyway, Javi does miracles with hair. And no offence, but Grace, we need a miracle to fix your hair."

"None taken. My frizz needs looking after." I pat my frizz before averting my eyes to Javi. "Do what you need to do. Just fix it."

Javi smiles. "It would be my pleasure."

*   *   *

As we enter Javi's hair salon, my jaw drops. Everything is so clean and organized, it looks like something out of a brochure. It smells of yummy hair products.

Javi indicates to a seat and quickly places a black cape around me. I sit down and glance at my reflection in the mirror. If I had seen myself like this two months ago, I would have thought it was a different person. My face has slimmed, making my blue eyes look larger and rounder like pools.

My acne has completely cleared up too, due to my new eating routine and new-found motivation for self-care.

My eyes look wide and bright. Looking back at it, being fat made everything look out of proportion.

Javi's voice snaps me out of my trance. "So, Grace, what color are you going for?"

"Anything but this. Give it a richer color. It just seems dull and frizzy no matter what I do to it."

"I am thinking of dying it a lighter brown and then some blonde highlights to give it a nicer color," he tells me. I have no objection so he gets to work. He clearly knows more than me.

"How would you like it cut, Grace?" Javi asks me as he begins to wash my hair.

"In a way where it isn't frizzy. Also, maybe something less . . . plain," I tell him, trying not to be unhelpful.

"I will start out by giving your hair a trim, because honey, it needs it." He winks at me in the mirror making me laugh. He's just like Jacob. "Then, I'll do the highlights and blow dry it. Sound good, Chica?"

I nod and let him get to work on my hair.

He begins to work with the scissors and only trims it so it still remains long, just above the small of my back. He then puts some layers in and shapes it around my face.

It all starts to get confusing when he starts applying the dyes. He mixes several colors together and I lose track of what he's doing. I close my eyes and relax. Who would have thought getting your hair done was exhausting?

After about half an hour, Javi places a weird machine over my head. Apparently, it's to make the highlights develop faster. I wouldn't know. I'm clueless when it comes to hair.

After another half an hour, he takes the machine off my head and then begins to dry my hair. He explains to me what he's doing as he does it so I can do it before school, in an attempt to look nice every day. I have to look my best every day if I want my revenge plan to work, right?

"Et voila!" Javi cheers, swinging my chair around to face the mirror.

My jaw drops. Stereotypical as it may sound, the girl in the mirror cannot be me. It can't be. Smooth, silky hair with the color of caramel and highlights of a creamy blonde tumble down my back in loose curls. The style frames my face, making me look delicate and . . . pretty?

Jacob and Amber come into the room and look to me. Jacob's jaw drops, leaving him speechless.

"Where is Grace and what have you done with her?" Amber demands with a joking tone. Javi chuckles and shrugs, unsure of what to say.

"Grace, you're hot!" Amber exclaims. "Like super-hot. Like Hailey Baldwin hot." I redden and shrug. Sure, I look a lot better than I did before but saying I'm on the same level as a model is a little far-fetched.

"Anyway, you girls should head home. Amber has something planned for you, haven't you babe?" Jacob says, waggling his eyebrows. Good god, I thought it was over?

"Sure, we'll see you back at the house." Amber blows Jacob a kiss, before turning away and strutting out of the door. My best friends are such divas.

TEN

When we arrive home, Mom is cooking in the kitchen, ensuring my fat girl greed is ignited. She does a double take as we enter the kitchen.

"Grace?" She scans my face, her voice full of confusion.

"I had my hair done, Mom. It's nothing that dramatic." I sigh. She sighs and smiles.

"It suits you. I also have some fantastic news." She grins and I know it must be something Dad related. "Your father is coming home later tonight!"

My mouth drops open in surprise. "Oh my god!" I squeal and rush over to give her a hug.

"Just remember, he's bringing that trainee that I told you about in July. He'll be sleeping in the spare room?" She says it like she's asking for approval. I grab an apple and shrug. I'm slightly bothered by it but I let it pass.

"Sure. Amber and I are going upstairs," I tell her and she flicks her hand at us. I think she's happy I finally have a friend. Amber grabs my hand and pulls me up the stairs.

"So, what awful thing have you got planned for me?" I ask her, falling onto the bed.

"I'm going to give you a makeup lesson!" She squeals, clapping her hands. I groan and place my head in my hands.

She pulls out two bags, both with the writing *MAC* on them. No, she didn't.

"I bought some makeup, all that you need. I got myself a new set while I was at it. Everything that you need is in here."

"You didn't have to, Ambs. I'm fine with what I've got."

"Mascara. That's it. I want you to learn the luxuries of makeup—the beauty of makeup," she says dramatically, making me chuckle. "Although I didn't buy any foundation since your skin already looks as if it's been airbrushed. Lucky devil." She smiles and pours out the contents of the bag onto my bed.

"Okay, to start with, you would usually use . . ." And that's where I lose her. From eyelash curling, to eyeliner flicking, to using bronzer to define my cheekbones, to applying lipstick in a specific way to stay in-trend, I can barely keep up.

But after she has gone through the tutorial and with effort, my makeup skills on myself improved. I am happy with the result.

The way she had showed me to apply eye shadow makes my blue eyes pop, and the cat-like flicks make my eyes seem more defined. And I don't know why I haven't used lipstick before, it does miracles for my lips. It makes them plumper and more 'kissable' as Amber rightly stated. Who wants to kiss a pair of thin, dry lips? No one. The exact reason why no guy has ever attempted to kiss me.

After blown kisses, exchanged hugs, and one hell of a long speech about school and clothes, Amber departs.

I collapse on my bed. A mentally exhausting day. I guess my revenge plan is ready to go? I shudder at the idea of having to pretend to be nice to Lucas. But I've got to if I want to pull this off.

Overcome with boredom and anticipation for dad to come home, I decide to see if the clothes from Paris fit. I grab a pair of skinny jeans and pull them up my legs. And as if it were some miracle, I don't have to wriggle too much to make them go over my thighs. And when buttoning them up, there is even a small gap for breathing room. This weight loss has really been miraculous.

I sort through the clothes and find a silky peplum top with lace hem and small jewels scattering the bottom section. I pull it over my head and find that it fits perfectly. I finish the outfit off with a light blue jacket, making my outfit sophisticated while also fitting the school code.

I check my outfit in the mirror. I like it a lot. My bedroom fashion show is cut off by the door slamming downstairs. It must be—

"Grace!" Mom calls. I groan and trundle down the stairs, not bothering to change my outfit. As I enter the living room, I see several bags scattering the room. He's barely even entered the room before I run at him with full speed.

"Dad!" I throw myself into his arms and hug him tightly. "Never go away ever again!"

I finally detach myself from him and he gives me a strange look.

"Grace? Is that you?" He holds me by my shoulders and examines me. I realize how different I must look to him. I'm a lot slimmer with new hair and makeup. No wonder he doesn't recognize me.

"Dad, I went on a diet. I lost weight and had my hair done," I explain and his face softens into a smile.

"Grace, you look absolutely beautiful. A model. I can't begin to explain how—" He is cut off by a thick Australian accent.

"Rob, where shall I put my stuff?"

And in walks the most attractive human being I've ever seen in my life. Dark hair, chiseled cheekbones, piercing blue eyes . . . mine being no match for his. He is tall with a strong, athletic build. Thank the Lord for letting the weather be warm today since all he's wearing is shorts and a tight white t-shirt, allowing me to see his defined abs. He must be a couple of years older than me if he's learning architecture. I remember Mom saying that he's twenty.

His eyes meet mine before raking his eyes over me and looks away. Not even a hello or a smile in greeting. He seems like the unfriendly type.

49

"Kaidan, meet Grace, my daughter. Grace, this is Kaidan," my dad introduces us, so I stick out my hand in order to be polite. Kaidan's eyes flicker over to me before looking away. He doesn't shake my hand. I step backwards, taken slightly aback. I frown and wait for an explanation. One doesn't come and I feel slightly embarrassed.

"I'm going to bed," I say. Before anyone can object, I hurry up the stairs and slam my door behind me.

Has that boy not heard of manners?

*　　*　　*

I wake up to the smell of bacon as per usual. Will got back from his holiday with his friends late last night, so Mom's probably decided to cook the family something nice to make a good impression on Mr. I-Have-No-Manners.

I trudge downstairs to see Will with his back to me. I rush up behind him and place my hands over his eyes.

He turns to face me with a grin on his face but it immediately drops.

"You changed your hair?"

"Yeah, is it better?" I ask, fiddling with a strand and twirling it around my finger.

"Sure, but I did love the frizz." He winks and then gestures for me to sit down next to him.

"How was Mexico?" I ask as I bite into a crispy red apple.

"Hot. And being in the legal age to drink?" He nudges me. "Eesh. That took it out of me." He laughs but it falters when Kaidan enters the kitchen.

"Who is that?" Will whispers as Kaidan casts a grumpy look over us. I narrow my eyes slightly before turning back to Kaidan.

"Dad is helping him with his first architecture practical. He's really grumpy," I say, but I'm not sure whether Kaidan hears me since he glances over at me with eyes full of hatred. Wow, what have I done to drive him round the bend?

Since I have one more day before school starts, I decide to only eat another apple because I'm able to put on weight as easily as a fat kid would give in to the temptation of chocolate.

Sighing, I get up from the table and wander through to the living room. I collapse onto the sofa and click the on button for the TV.

Suddenly, I feel someone sit down next to me. I glance over to see Kaidan who's staring straight ahead. I take the chance to really look at him. I mean really look at him. He has a small freckle to the left of his mouth and his eyelashes are thick and dark much like Javi's.

"Are you going to put the TV on or are you going to carry on staring at me?" he drawls, his Australian accent shining through the sarcasm. I blink once, twice, and a third time.

"I wasn't staring at you," I state as I choose a program to watch.

"Sure thing, Gracie."

"My name is Grace. Not Gracie." I clench my teeth together, annoyance hinting at my tone. He shrugs and turns back to the TV.

"I prefer Gracie."

"Well then go find someone who actually has the name Gracie," I snap, running my fingers through my hair. He glances over at me with a blank expression.

"Are you seriously watching this?" he asks. It takes me a while to realize he's talking about the TV show.

"Yeah. I am, actually," I say stubbornly. An unsatisfactory look passes over his face.

"Can you change it?" he demands. I look over at him with a blank expression.

"Look, Kiden, I know—"

"It's Kaidan," he corrects.

51

"Whatever. I know you're Australian and you may have different views on manners but here, you don't come marching into someone's house acting like you own the place," I say, folding my arms. Go Grace! I congratulate myself for being able to stand up to someone.

"Look Gracie, I know you're American and you may have different views on TV shows, but in Australia, we normally choose good TV shows to watch," he responds, mimicking me. I smile at him sarcastically.

"Whatever, Kris." I wave my hand dismissively.

"It's Kaidan." He corrects with annoyance edging his voice.

"Sure thing, Fabio. You can watch what you want, I'm not staying in here any longer." And with that I stand up.

"I said, my name is Kaidan."

"Bye Kyle." I wave my hand and march out of the room, anger coursing through me.

*　　*　　*

"Who does he think he is? Marching into our house and acting like a complete idiot, treating me like a piece of dirt? He just aggravates me to the end of the earth, and I haven't even known him for a day!" I yell into the phone.

"I'm sure he's not too bad," Amber says unsympathetically. I groan.

"He's awful Amber! He just makes me want to—" I'm suddenly cut off by a knocking on the door. I shuffle over and open it to see Kaidan standing there with a smirk on his face.

"I make you want to what, Gracie?" he asks, chuckling. I hear Amber say something inappropriate, but I ignore her.

"My name is Grace, Kiden," I say with gritted teeth. He just smirks.

"And mine is Kaidan."

"Same thing." I wave my hand dismissively and shut the door on his smug face. I pull my phone back up to my ear. "See? He's a complete douchebag!" I exclaim.

"I can hear you!" Kaidan shouts through the shut door. I ignore him.

"Grace, relax. Sure, he seems like an idiot but it takes two to tango. Be nice to him and he'll be nice to you." I want to punch her for playing devil's advocate!

"Yeah, that's how Americans play it, but in Australia, I'm not so sure." I rub the back of my neck and close my eyes. "But ever since he arrived, he's been nothing but nasty. Sure, he's nice to look at but his personality sucks," I say with a grumpy tone. I hear Amber sigh.

"Tell me about it tomorrow. I'll meet you by the school gates and we can walk through together, okay?" she asks. The idea of facing Lucas tomorrow fills my stomach with dread.

I gulp. "Sure, I'll see you there."

ELEVEN

Nerves wrack through me as we wait outside the looming school gates. Sure, being fat and bullied made school a hell hole but this is on a new level.

"Grace, stop worrying. You look gorgeous," Will says encouragingly. I shake my head and a feeling of nausea rushes through me.

"I can't do this."

"Yes, you can!" he says and pushes me out of the car. I smooth down the peplum top and jeans. *You've got this, Grace.* The little voice in my head encourages me. I want to yell at it because I definitely have not got this.

I take a small breath in an attempt to get rid of any negative thoughts and walk over to meet Amber by the gates. She squeals and pulls me in for a hug.

"Grace, you look amazing!"

I mumble a thank you as we walk through the school gates and into the main building.

To put it plainly, eyes are on me. At first, it arouses memories of when I used to be stared at and mocked for being fat. But now, it's different. The eyes on me are approving, not looking at me in disgust. They move up and down my body, and I even hear some mutters of 'Who's that chick?'

Amber tugs at my arm and we steer into our individual home rooms, blowing kisses as she wishes me good luck. I spot

Jacob immediately who wolf whistles as I make my way over to him.

"You look fab, Grace." He winks at me and I give him my best grin in an attempt to hide my nerves.

And that's when Lucas comes in. Surrounded by his minions, you would think he was the king of this school. My nerves develop into manic butterflies in my stomach with my hands growing damp. I keep my head down. I'm not ready to face him yet.

His feet stop and he places his hand on my desk. Dammit. "Hey," he says confidently. I look up and smile at him but I don't respond, mainly because my nerves are stopping me from doing so.

"Are you new around here?" he asks, his voice deep and alluring. I peer up at him through my eyelashes and take a deep breath. I spent my entire summer preparing for this moment. This is game on, Lucas Keith. Revenge time.

"No."

His expression is priceless. "Oh really? I've never seen you around. And I wouldn't miss a pretty face like yours," he says. I tuck a strand of hair behind my ear and sit upright, hoping to allude to confidence.

"Are you sure you don't recognize me, Lucas?" I taunt.

"You obviously know who I am. But what's your name?" he asks.

"Remember that fat girl who you used to bully?" I ask him in an innocent voice. He snorts.

"Grace Connely? I was wondering where she'd gone. I don't spot her though and well, she's hard to miss." He winks, as if we have some sort of inside joke. I keep my face straight.

"She's sitting in this room. Don't you see her?" I ask, biting my blue painted nail. His eyes scan the room.

"Nope."

"Surely she's too fat to miss?" I ask. He scans the room again, before his eyes land on me and his face drains.

"No, you can't be . . ." His expression grows pained and he stumbles backwards. I hold my hand out in satisfaction.

"My name is Grace," I say triumphantly. "I would say it's lovely to meet you but it seems we already know each other quite well." He looks down at my hand in shock but doesn't take it.

"What happened?" he asks, running a hand through his hair.

"People change. But personalities don't. It seems like you haven't changed one bit," I say, raking my eyes up and down his body. His face reddens.

"Look, Grace, I never meant any of that stuff. I was just teasing," he says nervously. Bingo.

"No, I'm pretty sure that was all real. I never took it to heart anyway." I wave my hand dismissively.

"Grace, you're overreacting. The only reason I ever did that was because I was jealous of you," he says, his face reddening even more. I snort. Is that really the best he can do?

"Jealous of me? Are you serious? Jealous of what? My ability to make chairs break and manage to get the whole of our grade laughing at me?" I ask, my memory flashing back to that awful day.

"Of your brains. You're so clever," he says and I almost burst into laughter. Not a great excuse, is it?

"I don't care. I'm over it," I say smirking. He sighs and closes his eyes.

"Please, Grace, forgive me. I can't begin to explain how sorry I am." His eyes are full of sorrow and embarrassment. Sucks to be you, buddy.

"Show me. Show me how sorry you are. Show me that my looks aren't the only reason you changed your mind about me." I'm lying, because there is no way that I will ever forgive him. But he doesn't have to know that, does he?

"How?"

"You'll think of a way. Bye, Lucas. Run along to your little friends." I push his stomach and he stumbles backward. With shock written all over his face, he returns to his friends. All of them sharing the same shocked look on him.

Sweet, sweet revenge.

*　　*　　*

The rest of the day runs pretty smoothly. Lucas smiles at me every time he sees me but I return with a straight face. He's not getting the easy way out.

It isn't until trig when Lucas approaches me again. Even though I'm seated at the front, he sits next to me. He pivots his seat so he's closer to me. I look over to him with a tired look.

"Hey Grace." He gives a small wave and I roll my eyes.

"Lucas, I'm seriously not interested, not after—"

"Can we just be friends? Please? I want to show you how sorry I am," he says. I roll my eyes.

"Who wants to be friends with someone who constantly made their life suck?" I ask, twirling a piece of hair around my finger.

"Give me a chance," he pleads. Before I can respond, someone steps in between us and stops.

"Leave her alone or I'll make you," says Pete. I look up to see the familiar furrowed eyebrows. His face is pure anger.

"Who are you?" Lucas asks, his voice hard as steel. I wince. This isn't going to go down well.

"Does it even matter?" Pete asks, smirking. For someone I barely know, I'm confused why he's standing up for me but I'm not complaining.

"Yeah, because you're trying to make me go away from my friend. If I want to sit here, I'll sit here." Lucas folds his arms, his large muscles bulging through his right fitted tee. Pete raises an eyebrow.

57

"Your friend? You are Lucas Keith, right? I'm pretty sure you bullied Grace for her entire time here at Jistie. But please, correct me if I'm wrong," Pete asks, towering over Lucas.

"I've already explained that I'm sorry for that." Lucas lowers his eyes, looking embarrassed again. Satisfaction seeps through me.

"Just go Lucas. Do yourself a favor and just go," Pete demands.

Lucas looks over at me with eyes filled with embarrassment and sadness. I cock my head to one side and smirk at him. That's what you get, asshole.

Pete settles down next to me. I look at him and as we gain eye contact, I look away, butterflies swarming in my stomach.

"Are you okay?" he asks me sincerely. I look up to him and nod slowly.

"Yeah. Thanks. You really didn't need to do that," I tell him, shocked that someone as attractive as him would be standing up for me. He shrugs.

"He's a shallow prick. I hate the guy. Gave me an excuse to put him in his place." He pauses before biting his lip. "You look really great, by the way."

A small smile makes its way onto my lips and I feel myself blushing. "Thanks. Um. You too."

TWELVE

When I return home from school the house is empty. I sigh in relief and hum a tune. That means I can go upstairs and—

"What are you doing?" says someone with an Australian accent. I mentally face palm and physically roll my eyes.

"Jeez, Kevin, I just got back from school." I look over to see he's sitting by the table, working on some architectural plan. Dad is nowhere to be seen. I frown. A muscle ticks in his jaw and his facial expression hardens.

"My name is Kaidan, Gracie," he says, his dark eyes meeting mine.

"And mine is Grace. Haven't we been through this?" I say, raising my eyebrows at him. "And where's my dad? Shouldn't you be working together?"

"He's gone to his office to get some plans. Can you go away? I'm trying to get this done before he gets back," he demands, flicking his pen at me. I give him a flat look.

"Kenneth, we've been through this. This is my house. You," I point my finger at him, "cannot tell me what to do."

"I swear Gracie, if you get my name wrong one more time, I'll—"

"You'll what, Kendrick?" My lips curve into a smile.

His face hardens. "You're unbelievable."

I can't help but burst out laughing. "Likewise."

"Whatever, Gracie. Leave me alone."

"If you hate me so much then why don't you just go back to Australia?" I ask him, my voice becoming more serious.

"I'm here to work. Trust me. I don't need some prissy teenage girl falling in love with me," he says, his face not changing one bit. I frown in shock. Well, someone has a big ego.

"Okay. Firstly, I'm not a prissy teenage girl. Secondly, why would you think I would fall in love with you? Lastly, I will never even like you in a million years. Capiche?"

"Wow, someone's a charmer," he says, his eyes wide. I narrow mine at him.

"I could say the same about you."

"I guess the feeling's mutual." His voice is deep and his dark lashes are lowered. "I'm not being rude, I'm just trying to work in peace."

"Well, you've done a great job on making me think so. Care to enlighten me? Do you have something against me or is this some twisted way of making friends?" I ask sarcastically.

"Just go away, Gracie." His eyes close and he breathes out deeply.

"My point exactly."

"Just leave me alone," he says sharply, his dark eyes meeting mine in an intense glare. I take a step back.

"Jeez, Kanye, take a chill pill." I pull my top lower on my stomach to prevent any flesh showing. His eyes dart to where my hands are before sliding back up to my face, anger written all over his expression.

"My name is Kaidan," he says through gritted teeth. I laugh.

"The more it annoys you, the more I'll do it."

"Just go away, Gracie." His voice is tired and his facial expression is weaker. "Let me get on with my work."

"Fine, see you later Karlos." I wave my hand and turn away. As I leave the room, I hear Kaidan make a small grunt of frustration.

All the anger pent up inside me arises as I enter my bedroom. I throw my bag onto the floor and its contents pool onto the soft carpet. I groan in frustration and pick up every pen and pencil.

I feel tempted to go to the gym out of habit so I change into shorts and a sports bra, chucking a big hoodie from my fat days and rushing down the stairs.

Kaidan is still working on the table, his head down and eyebrows furrowed. Horrible personality aside, good god that boy is attractive. If only . . .

I stop staring at him before he looks up and makes a snide comment about me 'falling in love with him.' He looks up at me and his gaze rakes my body. I decide wearing shorts may have been a bad idea.

"Where are you going?" he asks without a hint of anger in his voice this time.

"Just the gym," I tell him, pulling my hoodie down as long as I can.

"Why?" he asks me with a puzzled look on his face.

"Same reason everyone goes to the gym—to work out." I shrug, not wanting him to know about my weight loss. He looks at me intently before returning his gaze down to the sheets of paper.

"Where is it?" he asks, his eyes low. I shrug.

"It's nearby. Look it up," I tell him, shrugging for the fourth or fifth time.

"You shrug a lot," he says. I give him a confused look because his eyes are on the paper he's working on.

"You're not even looking at me, Kameron."

Now he looks up, anger etched across his face again. "Kaidan. My name is Kaidan, Gracie."

"And mine is Grace. I'm getting a sense of déjà vu here." I smirk. He gives me a sarcastic smile before dismissing me. I notice that it is warm outside, so I decide on doing something bold.

I pull the large hoodie over my head and toss it at Kaidan. He looks at me in awe, having seen my sports bra. Confidence surges through me, and a small smile tugs at my lips.

"Bye Kale." I wiggle my fingers at him before marching out of the door. Once I'm out of the door, I grin widely.

The sun beats down on my bare arms and stomach. Grinning even more, I turn my quick walking into a jog, eager to get to the gym.

I notice a boy walking on the other side of the road. He looks over in my direction and I realize it's Lucas. I mentally face palm. He must live really near me. What joy.

He sends me a grin and quickly jogs across the road to meet me. His eyes scan over my body before meeting my eyes.

I suddenly regret my earlier decision and wish my hoodie was covering my bare flesh.

"Hey, Grace." He flashes his dazzling whites at me. "You going to the gym?"

"Yeah, I am. If you'd excuse me . . ." I try to walk past him, but he places his warm hand on my shoulder to stop me. My eyes dart down to where his fingers are on my tanned skin. My shoulders tense. His eyes meet mine.

"You look good, Grace," he mumbles. My head jerks up and I take a step away from him.

"I need to go." But my words come out as a croak. I clear my throat and attempt to walk past him again. His hand stops me but this time he places it on my waist.

I smack his arm and shove past him, my shoulder grazing his. "Leave me alone."

He smirks. "Okay, sweet cheeks. Have it your way."

*   *   *

62

My deep breathing is the only thing I can hear. The gym is pretty much empty and Amber isn't here since she only works on weekends during school time. A muscly man picking up weights is the only other person here. His face is red and sweat drips down his face.

My steps become quicker as I turn the pace up on the running machine. The door creaks open, and someone walks in. Thank god. Now I won't have to be alone with Mr. Red Face.

"Can I buy a membership, please?" an Australian-sounding voice says. My blood turns to ice. Why is he here?

I find myself wiping the sweat from my forehead and pulling my hair out of its tight ponytail. I don't want him to see me like this. Maybe I'm as red as Mr. Red Face.

He makes his way towards me but I keep my eyes focused on a chip in the wall. I pretend I didn't see him and keep my pace fast.

He steps onto the treadmill beside mine and begins to run. Dammit. I feel tempted to move onto another machine but the way his head pivots to look at me, I know he's going to start a conversation.

"Your face is really red," he says. Well, duh. At least the redness of my embarrassment won't change to give him any more satisfaction.

"Why are you here, Kazz?" I look over at him. His eyes avoid mine as he presses a couple of buttons on his machine. I see his jaw harden. He's agitated, I can tell.

"For the same reason as yours," he says plainly.

Well, unless you used to be a fat pig and decided to lose weight, you're probably not, I think to myself. I stifle a giggle. He looks over at me with a puzzled expression.

"What are you laughing at?" he asks. His breathing has become quicker as he's beginning to get tired out.

"Nothing."

Silence falls between us and we stay this way for ten minutes. That is, until Kaidan steps off his machine and pulls his t-shirt over his head. My jaw drops open.

Sweet Mary, Joseph and baby Jesus in a manger.

His stomach is lined with strong, lean abs. They tense as he places his t-shirt on the floor. I close my mouth before he can see.

He looks over at me. "What? I'm hot," he says.

Yes, you are. I say to myself. The innuendo almost makes me laugh, although I don't think he realizes what he said.

He wanders over to the weight lifting station to join Mr. Red Face. I can't help but stare at his back as he walks away.

I mean, for goodness sake, who actually looks like that? I gulp, before turning away and switching my machine off. I try not to look at him as I cross over to the cycling machine.

His arm muscles ripple as he lifts the weights. I feel giddy. He is a gift from the gods. As I watch him, I realize that he'd probably be able to lift me. Imagine that.

He suddenly sits up and rubs his wrists. I turn away and focus on the aching in my legs. I feel his gaze on me and I pump my legs harder. I blink and turn my head slowly. Our eyes meet and I see him smirk. I return it before adjusting the side of my sports bra. His eyes dart down to my chest before sliding up to meet mine.

I smirk and switch off the machine, pulling my leg over and jumping off the high seat. I turn away and grab my bag. I walk out of the door and the male receptionist gives me an approving look. I turn back and see Kaidan with a look filled with . . . anger?

I smile at him and walk out the door.

THIRTEEN

I arrive home to loud voices and groan. Will has friends over. I tiptoe through the kitchen and dart up the stairs. Thankfully, they didn't see me wearing sweaty, revealing clothes.

I strip my clothes off immediately and hurry into the bathroom, eager to clean the stink of the gym off me as soon as possible.

After a long wash, I climb out of the shower and wrap a soft towel around me. Humming, I wander out of the bathroom and walk casually into my bedroom.

I walk into a wall, and the wall gives way. Wait, nope. Walls don't make noises. Or have hands that are now around my waist.

I squeak and look up, seeing a very confused looking Kaidan. My cheeks grow hot and I take a step back from him.

His hands are still on my waist.

"What are you doing, Gracie?" he asks.

"I, I . . . I wasn't looking where I was going . . . sorry," I mumble, my cheeks as red as they've probably ever been. His pressure on my hips is looser but he still holds them.

"I need to go. I'm feeling seriously revealed," I say laughing. He nods and releases me.

"Don't be too clumsy, Gracie," he says in all seriousness.

"Don't count on it, Kyden," I say with a light-hearted tone. Yet he still stares at me with that intensity, his eyebrows furrowed.

Does that boy ever smile?

Now I sit in trig, my pencil twirling around my finger effortlessly. Yesterday's events left me in a fluster and I decided to not emerge from my room so I wouldn't have to face Kaidan. I got up especially early today to avoid him. The fact that he saw me with dripping wet hair in my pink towel was a little too much for me to cope with.

I suddenly feel a pen prod me in the back. I swivel in my chair and see Pete smiling at me. I smile back. "Hey."

"How's Lucas? Need me to beat him up for you?" he jokes, his eyes crinkling at the corner. Wow. He really is gorgeous. I silently thank God for placing two gorgeous guys into my life at the same time, although Pete is a whole lot nicer than Kaidan.

"I think I'm okay at the moment but I'll let you know." I laugh with him before spying Jacob hovering at the corner of the classroom, a knowing look on his face. I beckon him over, because I know exactly what he's thinking.

"Hey guys." He winks at me and takes the seat next to Pete. "What are you laughing at?"

"Lucas," we say in unison, before breaking into laughter again. Jacob raises his eyebrows at me but I just ignore him. I'll let his imagination go wild.

Trig commences and we are shushed by the teacher. We fall into silence but I can't stop smiling. My very first crush. On someone I think may even like me back.

My thoughts are confirmed when Pete taps my shoulder. I turn around subtly to avoid getting into trouble with the teacher.

"Wanna get a milkshake at the diner after this?" he asks me and I grin before nodding. I think that Pete may definitely like me back.

*   *   *

"Two Oreo milkshakes, please," Pete orders for both of us. Part of me wants to order a smoothie because I know how easy it'll be to fall into my old eating patterns but I leave it because I think I am on a date (emphasis on the think).

When our milkshakes arrive, we make our way over to a booth.

"Here you go." Pete passes me my milkshake and I thank him once again for paying for it.

"No problem." He takes a sip of his. "I just want to say, I think it's really amazing what you did over the summer."

I forgot he knew what I looked like before my weight loss. "Thank you. It was hard, that's for sure."

He nods and sips his drink once more. "I bet. And part of the reason Lucas angers me so much is because he drove you to do that to yourself." Pete burrows those dark eyebrows of his. "I think he's an awful human being."

"I agree that he's not very nice. But he gave me the motivation to lose weight, to make myself healthy." I bite my lip. "And in some twisted way, I guess I'm thankful for that."

"Twisted, that's for sure." Pete chuckles, but there isn't much amusement behind it. I can tell how much he hates Lucas. He doesn't even need to put it into words.

"Don't get me wrong, I hate his guts. He hit me, for Christ sake." I shudder at the memory and it reignites my hatred. Hitting a girl? That's lower than low. Even for Lucas.

"He hit you?" Pete chokes on his words. I nod awkwardly. Pete curses under his breath and looks up to me.

"You don't deserve that." He swears again. "Next time I see that son of a bitch, I swear to God . . ."

"It's in the past, Pete. It's fine," I tell him but really, it's not fine.

And so, I realize that I need to step into a higher gear in this revenge plan. There's no taking it easy anymore.

FOURTEEN

I walk into the kitchen to see Will and Dad eating at the table.

"Had a good evening?" Will asks. I told him I was going out with Amber, you know, because of the whole protective big brother thing going on.

"Yeah, it was good," I say, before rushing upstairs. My face glares red when I lie. Best not to let him know I went out with a boy.

"Where have you been?" comes a voice when I enter my room. To my shock, I see Kaidan lying on my bed reading my diary. I gasp and snatch it from him.

"What are you doing in my room?" I shout. He winces and smirks, sitting up and patting the patch of bed next to him.

"Waiting for you to get back," he simply says. What the?

"You were . . ." I don't finish my sentence because he cuts me off.

"So, where have you been?"

"Out," I reply, still curious why he's wondering. He raises an eyebrow at me, those cool eyes boring into mine.

"Funny, I heard you say you were out with Amber. I saw her working out at the gym," he says.

"What is this, an Inspector Calls? Chill out. I was having dinner with a friend." I wave my hand dismissively, hoping he will leave. But he remains lying on my bed and I want to punch him.

"A friend? Or a . . ." He winks. "A frriiieeennnddd."

I groan. What is he, twelve years old? "Why do you care?" I ask. He shrugs.

"I don't, to be honest. Just curious. And mainly because Amber told me you were on a date." He shrugs, the cold, empty eyes returning. Dammit, I should have never texted her!

He spoke to Amber?

"You spoke to her? Why?" I ask, curiosity surging through me.

"Well, I heard her register and tell the man at the desk her name was Amber. I knew you had a friend called Amber, so I decided to talk to her," he says with a nonchalant tone.

My jaw drops. This guy can't be for real.

"Anyway, I can tell by the way she was looking at me. She thought I was a total eye candy." He winks at me.

"She must be blind," I say casually, looking away in case my face blares red due to lying.

"Oh Gracie, don't talk like that. I saw you staring at me in the gym," he says in a low voice. Heat of embarrassment courses through me, but I push it to one side.

"Likewise," I say, folding my arms across my chest. Go Grace!

"I was not staring at you," he says, sighing at the end, his features slacking, erasing any humor behind his eyes.

"I can tell by the way you were looking at me. You thought I was a total eye candy," I mimic him, and I see him roll his eyes.

"God, Gracie. Anyone with a pair eyes can acknowledge that," he says. My eyes widen and then his do, suddenly realizing what he's said.

"What?" I gasp.

"What?" he replies, his eyes still wide. He runs his hand through his dark hair, ignoring what just happened, his eyes are wide, so different to their normal ice cold, hard stare.

69

"You think I'm eye candy?" I ask in a teasing tone. He chuckles in a low voice. The first time I've heard him laugh, I swear.

"As I stated, yeah, you're not bad looking. Just because I can acknowledge that, doesn't mean I'm in love with you, okay? Just take the compliment," he says, deflecting any affection that he was showing towards me.

"I'm sorry if I can notice when you're not acting like the arrogant jerk you normally are." I narrow my eyes at him. He puts his hands up in surrender and stands up.

"I guess I won't give you a compliment any time soon." He raises an eyebrow. "And also, I love the comments in your diary about me. I may be a jerk, but your swirly pink pen begs to differ." He winks and swaggers out of the room.

My face blares red and I snatch the diary and look at the page it's open on.

> Dear diary,
> God, some new kid called Kaidan arrived today. He's a right jerk!
> But so damn attractive though. Why? Ugh.

I slam my palm into my face in embarrassment. I shut the diary and groan in frustration, watching him as he walks out of my room. I don't even have to be able to see his face to know that his mouth is pulled up in a smirk.

*   *   *

Late for school again, I rush into home room in complete exhaustion. Kaidan decided it would be funny to turn my alarm off. And so, I woke up later, with no time for makeup or hair. Which explains the wrecked state I'm in right now. Jacob glances at me from his seat and gapes at me.

70

"Honey, what happened?" he asks me with wide eyes. I want to reply, but before I can say anything, a certain blonde-haired boy steps in front of me.

"Grace, how are you?" Lucas beams at me. I sigh, then stop when I realize I haven't brushed my teeth.

"Can't you tell?" I gesture to the state I'm in. Lucas' gaze travels over me before shaking his head.

"I think you look great." A smile doesn't budge from his lips.

"Well, thanks, but I know you're saying that to get bonus points," I say, before swiveling round and sitting down at my desk. I see Jacob sniggering in the corner of my eye but I choose to ignore him. I comb my fingers through my hair in an attempt to calm the frizz. Unfortunately, it seems only a hair dryer can tame the mane.

After home room, I remember the pact I made with myself when I was on the date with Pete. Step it up a gear. I take a deep breath and turn to Jacob.

"Okay, I'm about to say something and I need you to say no, okay?" I whisper to him.

He frowns at me in confusion and I just wink at him.

"Hey Jacob, want to get a milkshake with me after school?" I say loudly so that Lucas can hear. "I'm craving one of those milkshakes."

Jacob is still frowning at me like I've lost my mind. I kick him under the table. "Um," he squints his eyes at me. "No?" He seems unsure and I fight back a giggle. "No, I'm busy." He sounds surer this time and I praise my best friend for finally catching on.

"Damn." I sigh and just like clockwork I hear Lucas clear his throat.

Bingo.

"I'll go with you if you want?" he asks, moving into the seat next to me. I look his way and pretend to consider his offer for

71

a moment. I can see Jacob attempting to work out my plan. Just you wait and see.

"I don't know, Lucas . . ." I bite my lip and shrug.

"Just give me this one chance, please?" he pleads with those big brown eyes and I realize in this moment why so many girls fall for his charm.

Not me though.

"Fine. I'll meet you there at 4 p.m." I turn my attention back to the class. Revenge time.

*　　*　　*

Ring!

The bell marks the end of class. As we leave the room, Jacob grabs my arm and pulls me into a supply closet.

"Woah, I didn't realize I was your type." I chuckle as he pins me up against the wall. He shakes his head at me.

"Want to tell me what that was about?" he asks. "You're not seriously going on a date with Mr. I-Hit-Girls, are you?"

"Relax," I tell him, pushing his arms off me. "Of course not. I just want to embarrass him, that's all." Realization floods through his features.

"Thank god. I was about to get Amber in to give you a serious pep talk." He folds his arms. "So, what's your plan?"

"Stand him up, basically. He goes at four, waits half an hour, then we rock up. I'll pretend I didn't know about the date," I tell him. Not the most genius plan, but it will work all the same.

"So . . . do I get a milkshake out of this or not?" Jacob asks, a smirk on his face.

I shake my head and giggle. "You're impossible."

*　　*　　*

The end of the day comes around fairly quickly and soon enough Jacob, Amber, and I are crouching outside the diner waiting for Lucas to show up. The moral part of my mind is telling me that I shouldn't humiliate a person like this but then I remember what he did to me. And that he deserves it.

"This is brilliant!" Amber squeals and squeezes my arm. "I've been waiting so long to see him get what he deserves," she says evilly and I give her a sideward look. She shrugs. "Hey, he was a dick to me too, okay? This is just as exciting for me."

I spot Lucas getting out of his car. "There he is!" I whisper. We all shrink lower so that he can't see us. He saunters into the diner like he owns the place before taking a seat at a booth.

And now we wait.

The first ten minutes are pretty dull as far as revenge plans go. Lucas just sits and waits, probably assuming I'm running late. He begins to grow impatient fifteen minutes in, drumming his fingers on the table and checking his phone incessantly.

"When do we go in?" Amber asks, popping a lollipop into her mouth.

"Just a little longer." I keep my eyes on him, hoping that he won't just give up and leave. The diner is filling up with people from Jistie High, meaning the event will probably be broadcast to the entire school in a matter of minutes.

The waitress walks over to Lucas' table and asks him something. He shakes his head and gestures to the seat next to him. He's telling her he's waiting for someone, little does he know.

I check my watch to see that half an hour has passed, and it's time for step two of my brilliant plan.

"Let's go," I tell the others. We walk into the diner as casually as we can, arms linked. I can tell that eyes are on us from the whispering around us. We sit in the first booth that we come to, in the perfect position for Lucas to spot us. But he already has and is storming up to the table just as we take our seats.

73

"What the hell, Grace?" His cheeks are red with frustration. I mock confusion and frown at him.

"Woah, what's up?" I ask him, keeping my laughter at bay. He runs his hands through his hair angrily.

"You know exactly what's up. We were supposed to meet up for a milkshake, remember?" he snaps at me. I deepen my frown and shake my head.

"I don't know what you're talking about. I had plans with Jacob and Amber hence I'm here with them," I tell him slowly.

"That's bullshit and you know it!" he shouts and I flinch. "You stood me up, Grace."

"Lucas, I'm being serious. I have no idea what you're talking about." I shrug. "You can join us if you want." I gesture to the seat next to me.

"I'm fine, thanks," he spits, before turning his gaze to Amber. "I bet this is your doing. You're still bitter about the break up, aren't you? Manipulating Grace into hating me?"

Amber sucks on her lollipop silently and I fight the urge to laugh.

"Lucas, you know what? You're right." She cocks her head to one side. "I am still bitter about the break up. But I didn't manipulate Grace into hating you, honey. You did that all by yourself." She pops her lollipop back into her mouth before making a sweeping motion with her hands.

Lucas looks so angry that he's about to explode but instead, he just turns around and storms out of the diner. It's then that I notice the entire diner is not empty and several phones recorded the entire thing.

And that, folks, is how it's done.

FIFTEEN

When I arrive home, Will isn't around. Probably being mobbed by his thousands of admirers. Someone is home though and it can't be Mom. She's working late hours tonight since there was a compulsory fashion show she was required to cover. God, being a fashion writer must be hard. Dad is at work and so does Kaidan. So, who's cooking? I hang up my coat and kick my shoes off before shuffling around the corner. I peer to see who is cooking.

Holy mother of god.

Kaidan is standing at the stove, a towel slung loosely around his hips. His lean, tan body is in its full glory, tensing as he prods the food in the pan.

I lean further to look at him more closely before tripping and falling flat on my face. The loud bang causes him to turn around in surprise.

"What happened?" Kaidan asks, his eyes wide. I push myself up, and feel my face redden.

"I tripped," I say, before slicking my hair back in an attempt to tame the frizz.

"Okay . . ." he says, uncertainty clear in his tone. I give him a sheepish smile and walk lamely over to the stove.

"Where's Dad?" I ask him. He turns over whatever he's cooking in the pan and looks over at me.

"He sent me home from the office early. He has an external client so I get the afternoon off." He smirks and turns his attention back to the food. I look into his pan to see a whole pizza in the center of it.

"Why the hell are you frying a pizza?" I ask him with wide eyes. He chuckles and removes the pan from the stove and slides the pizza onto a plate.

"Why not?" He raises an eyebrow at me. I roll my eyes.

"You know, Kyle, you're too cocky for your own good." I grab an apple and watch irritation contort his features.

"You know, Gracie, you keep getting my name wrong." He frowns. "And you eat too healthily. Let go and pig out for once in your life," he says.

I'm about to object but I realize one unhealthy thing won't do any damage.

"Sure, why not." I shrug and follow him into the TV room. I plop down on the sofa and tuck my legs underneath me.

"Your hair is frizzy today, you look like a kitten," he says casually, before taking a bite of his pizza.

"A kitten?"

"Like a baby cat?" he says, stating the obvious.

I roll my eyes again. "I don't look like a kitten," I say, frustration lacing my tone.

"You're like a little fuzzy kitten and you think you're so fierce, but you're not." He takes another slice of pizza and puts it in his mouth.

I gape at him. First, he calls me Gracie and now I look like a kitten? What next, caterpillar? I sigh, then turn the TV on. I flick through the channels before finding *The Notebook* on, right at the start.

"We are not watching this, Gracie," he says in a bored tone. I am irritated by the nickname but I cool down and ignore him.

"Gracie?" he repeats. I turn my head to look at him.

76

"Look, Kristian, we're watching this no matter—" I rebut, but he cuts me off.

"It's fine, we'll watch it. But I was going to offer you a slice of pizza," he says, holding a slice out to me.

My mouth forms an 'O' and I take the slice he's offering me. I take a small bite gingerly but when I realize how good it tastes, I gulf down the rest.

"Alright, Fat Amy," he says laughing. I give him a look of disgust and turn my eyes back to the movie.

Halfway through the movie, I realize he's still only wearing a towel and I giggle.

"What are you laughing at?" he asks. I shake my head but he stares me down, those blue eyes threatening me.

"You're still only wearing your towel." I giggle and realization floods through his features, but then that oh-so-familiar smirk reappears on his face.

"Would I rather take it off?" he asks me, no hint of laughter on his face. He's surely winding me up.

"No, it's just . . ." I trail off, unsure of what to say.

"It's just what, Gracie?"

"Nothing, sit in your towel if it pleases you, Kris. Whatever floats your boat." I laugh and see a small smile on his lips, something so different from his usual smirk.

"I thought I was the only one home. It clearly bothers you, so I'll go and get changed." He huffs and stands up before wandering up to his room. I watch his tanned behind, a small part of me hoping the towel would fall down.

After a couple of minutes, Kaidan returns wearing sweatpants and a t-shirt. I think I preferred the towel.

Once Kaidan has settled on the sofa, we both turn our attention back to the TV and carry on watching the film, which eventually makes me have tears streaming down my face.

The credits roll down the screen and tears continue to roll down my cheeks. Kaidan thankfully hasn't noticed nor is he showing any emotion at the movie. God, does he have a heart made from stone?

I sniff, giving myself away.

Dammit.

"Gracie, what's wrong?" he asks.

Gee, Kaidan! I don't know, maybe we just watched the saddest film ever? I wipe the tears away with the back of my hand and give him a flat look. He raises his eyebrows in request for an explanation.

"Did you not find that sad?" I ask, sniffing. The small trace of worry that was on his face disappears and he smiles.

"Not really. Go get a tissue." He ruffles his hair before taking the remote and changing the channel.

Wow. Any emotion I saw flicker inside Kaidan is gone. The empty, cool eyes are back, with no heat behind them whatsoever.

He puts some strange TV show on and I drift off . . .

*　　*　　*

I open my eyes into slits before realizing the room is dark. I guess I fell asleep on the sofa while watching TV.

The second thing I realize is that Kaidan and I are basically wrapped around each other. My head is on his chest and his head is resting on me. My arm is draped around his bare torso and his is wrapped around my waist. Our legs are tangled up and his t-shirt is halfway up his chest. Hello, abs…

I move slowly, attempting to release myself from his tight hold. However, my movement wakes him up. He opens his eyes and looks down at me.

I smile sheepishly at him and it takes him a couple of seconds to process what he is doing. He suddenly removes his arm from around me and leaps up, pulling his t-shirt down as he does.

"Gracie, why were you sleeping on me?"

"Look pal, I wasn't the one with the viper grip around your waist." I shrug and his eyes widen.

78

"Sorry about that," he says, scratching the back of his head. God, I'm still not used to his physique.

"Is nobody home?" I ask before yawning. He watches me intently, not giving me an answer. Damn, do I have something on my face?

"Kaidan?" I ask, waving my hand in front of his face.

His eyes widen. "You got my name right," he says with a shocked look on his face. It's now my turn to be shocked. I should've held out for longer.

"Well, yeah, I guess . . ." I pause then snap my head up. "Does that mean you'll stop calling me Gracie?"

"Nope," he says with the infamous smirk on his face. I groan.

"Please?" I plead. He pretends to think for a bit but then shakes his head.

"No, it suits you." The coolness of his eyes fades a bit and I almost see a bit of emotion.

I puff out a breath of air in anger and push a stray curl of hair from my face. Damn curls.

"Anyway, this has been lovely but I'm going." He stands up. The sarcasm in his voice is painfully rigid.

I immediately shadow his movements. He gives me a strange look and I tuck a loose curl behind my ear.

"But where are you going?" The words are out of my mouth before I can stop them. I have no self-restraint, I swear.

"I need to do some work. I'm supposed to be working." He looks at me intensely with those blue eyes. The coolness is back and he gives me a look as if to say, 'This hasn't been a bonding experience. Leave it. We are not friends.'

I step back a little, startled. He pushes past me, his shoulder hard against mine. I don't turn around to watch him go. I just stand there, feeling like I've been slapped in the face. Maybe a slap would have been better.

SIXTEEN

My alarm bleeps. Thank god Kaidan didn't turn it off again. I pull myself out of bed and begin my routine. Shower. Blow dry hair. Brush teeth. Swipe on mascara.

I stare in the mirror and assess the outcome. I swear I look like a different person when I make an effort. I throw a pair of jeans on then a silk cami with ruffles. I smile at my reflection and wander downstairs. I see Kaidan and Will sitting together eating breakfast, laughing about something.

Wow. Kaidan laughing? A sight I thought I'd never see. I watch them with a small smile on my face. Kaidan's features are less intense. His eyes are less hard and friendlier, crinkled at the corners. The relaxed expression makes him look younger somehow. Even more gorgeous.

I push those thoughts out of my head and sit next to Will, as far away from Kaidan as possible.

"Morning," Will says, fluffing my hair. I smooth it down and see Kaidan pass an irritated look over me. Anger surges through me, and I slam my fist down on the table.

"What have I done wrong now?" I sigh. Those eyes look up at me, emotion free. As our eyes connect, however, I see an ounce of emotion. He cocks his head to the side and stares me down.

"Your hair looks nicer when you don't blow dry it," he says simply. Then he places his mug down on the table and stands up, the chair screeching against the kitchen floor as he does so.

I sit there with a gob smacked expression. I hear Will chuckle under his breath, so my eyes dart over to him.

"Give him a chance, Grace. He's a good guy." He takes a bite of a pop tart and raises his eyebrows at me. "Just spend some more time with him. Five minutes over breakfast and he'll loosen right up."

"Will, I've spent a lot more than five minutes with him. We had a full-on movie bonding time yesterday yet he still looks at me like he wants to kill me." I sigh and run my hands through my hair.

"I don't know. He's a couple years older. Maybe he feels uncomfortable. You're only seventeen after all."

"Nearly eighteen." I mumble grumpily. He laughs and fluffs my hair again.

I pour out a cup of orange juice and sip it quietly. As my eyes wander the room, I look at the mirror where I see the reflection of the living room where Kaidan stands, listening to every word of our conversation.

$$*\qquad*\qquad*$$

As soon as I walk through the school gates Amber bounces up to me like a puppy. I give her a small smile and she links our arms.

"Omigosh Grace, I have the best news," she says, speaking loudly into my ear. When she notices my grumpy expression, she frowns. "What's wrong?"

I raise an eyebrow at her and realization floods through her features.

"Kaidan," we say together, then burst into a fit of giggles.

"He is yumtastic by the way. With a cherry on top. When he came over and spoke to me, I thought I'd won the lottery. But then I realized he was your Kaidan and the only reason he was speaking to me was to get the juice about you." She picks at a perfectly manicured nail. I give her a flat look.

"He was so not asking about me."

"He so was, Grace. He even referred to you as 'my Gracie' which is totally adorbs." She sighs like it's a sweet gesture and I admit, butterflies erupt in my stomach. *My Gracie.*

"Well, what did he ask?" I ask in a bored tone.

"He firstly asked why you're so obsessed with being at the gym—"

I gasp and cut her off. "You didn't tell him, did you?"

"Course not, bubs. Told him you were just one of those girls who wanted to keep fit." She hesitates then continues. "Then he started asking if you were insecure and saying how you shouldn't be . . . it was like a news report," she finishes.

Thoughts in my head are seriously jumbled up. I push past them.

"Why would he think I was insecure?"

"I dunno Grace. Maybe because you live at the gym?"

I step back, stung by her words. Her eyes widen and she babbles out an apology. However, I tune out. Because all I can concentrate on are the things Kaidan asked about me.

"Anyway," she puffs out, stepping in front of me and placing her hands on my shoulders, "Jistie party, tomorrow. We're going." I feel my stomach drop. Jistie party equals Lucas and I still haven't him since the diner incident yesterday.

"I thought you only went to Cranbrook parties?" I raise an eyebrow at her. She laughs.

"Well, I have you to go with! Plus, Lucas will be there. It'll be funny." She swivels around to face me. "Also, Pete's going." She wiggles her eyebrows.

I swat her arm. "Shut up."

"He likes you!" She grabs my face with both her hands. "You should go out with him!"

82

"I did!" I exclaim. "But I've barely seen him since. I think he's avoiding me."

"Oh, come on. He hasn't. The reason you don't want to go out with him is very clear." She raises her eyebrows at me. I give her a blank expression.

"And what is that?" I fold my arms.

"You like Kaidan, duh!" She loops her arm around mine. I stop in my tracks and give her a wide-eyed look.

"Are you serious?" I frown. "There's no way I like him. I would even go as far as hating him. Why do you think I like him?" Amber rolls her eyes.

"He's the only thing you ever talk about. I know that when I talk about someone a lot. It means I'm into them." She gives me a knowing look.

"Well, you're wrong. I only talk about him because I find him annoying," I tell her and Amber nods. She definitely does not believe me.

"Whatever you say. But we are going to this party, plus it's Halloween, so we can get some killer costumes," she rambles. Classic Amber.

I sigh. "Fine. But I'm not wearing anything ridiculous."

*　　*　　*

Ridiculous didn't even begin to cover it. After wandering around the mall for what seemed like decades, we'd only found one outfit which Amber approved of. A small devil costume with a corset and a black ribbon framing it. It came with horns and a trident, and only came past her bum.

Feet aching, I drag myself into the next shop Amber chooses. "Grace, you have to choose something. This is the last shop," she says impatiently.

"Fine." I sigh, Amber squeals and drags me in. Among the witches, pumpkins, mice, rabbits, and demons, there is nothing I would call appropriate.

"Halloween is the best time to dress up! You can look like an idiot and no one will judge you," she says. I give her a dead look saying 'are you kidding me?'

Knowing Amber, she probably wasn't. I search through the shop until I see a costume that would cover most of me. High-waisted disco pants with a crossover crop top. A slice of my tummy will be on show, but nothing in comparison to the other costumes. Little cat ears and a tail come with it. Ok, I'll be a cat, settled. I pick up a size 6 and wander over to Amber.

She catches a look at the outfit and beams. "Seductive cat? Love it!" She peeks at the size. "Honey, there is no way you're a six. I'll go grab a two and you can try it on."

"Amber!" I shout out as she wanders off, but she's already gone. I am not a size two. I can't even squeeze into a four! I push my hands through my hair and wait for her to return. She skips up to me, snatches the six from my hand and pushes me into the changing room. I sigh and take the bag.

"Come out when you've got it on!" she calls, so I give her a nod and shut the door. I eye the costume as if my eyes will make it a size bigger. Or two.

I sigh and strip my clothes off then begin to pull the disco pants on. They squeeze my legs but continue up. I wiggle until they reach my waist, where I do them up. Huh. Perfect fit. I guess I've lost more weight now. A small smile is on my face. Never in my life would I have thought that I, Grace Connely, would be a size two. I pull on the crossover top, which also fits, probably due to the fact I've inherited a small chest from my mother. I pull down the top, attempting to cover the slither of tummy on display but failing miserably. I put on the cat ears and open the door. Amber stands there and as soon as she sees me, she beams.

"Omigosh Grace, you look hot!" she says and I hear a wolf whistle from across the shop. My eyes flicker over to a group of boys our age, all looking at me. I blush, and look back to Amber, who's nodding.

"What?" I ask. A mischievous look is on her face.

"Kaidan is gonna go crazy when he sees you in that." She licks her lips and smiles at me.

"You're crazy."

"You'll see."

*   *   *

The day of the party approaches too fast. Here I am, sitting in sweatpants, my hair a frizz, waiting for Amber to arrive and do my hair and makeup. The doorbell rings and before I can even stand up, Will has already answered the door.

I wander down and see him nervously shake his hair. Huh. I guess Amber has that effect on him.

"Yeah, so Grace and I are going to the Cranbrook party tonight." Amber pauses and sees me, launching towards me for a hug.

"Uh, Grace, can I talk to you?" Will says, pulling me to the side. I raise one eye brow at him in question.

"What?"

"You can't go to a Halloween party. I won't allow it," he says. "Not alone."

"I'll be with Amber duh," I say, "and Jacob."

"Just come to the one where I'll be at so I can keep an eye on you," he says.

"Um, no. You have fun with your friends and I'll have fun with mine," I tell him. "Plus, I'm pretty sure the guy that's hosting mine is like four houses down from yours. You can come and check on me if you really need to."

"Grace, come on," he says. I shake my head stubbornly.

85

"No, Will. No way," I say and he sighs.

"Grace, don't test me."

"No, you don't test me. You're not my father and I can do what I want. I'll go have fun with my friends while you go have fun with yours," I tell him, feeling superior.

"My friends can be your friends. Only one year apart, we're practically the same age," he says.

"No, Will. I hate being the tagalong." I fold my arms.

"But—"

I cut him off. "No buts. You're not going to persuade me."

"Fine, but I'm sending Kaidan with you then," he says.

"No way. Nuh uh. You must be joking?!" I say, gob smacked.

"No argument. See ya, Grace," he says. "No buts. You're not going to persuade me." He mocks me and winks, before swaggering off. I wipe my hands on my jeans and sigh. Hopefully, Kaidan will decline.

I return to Amber who's watching with wide eyes. I shake my head. "No comment," I say. She just laughs and follows me up to my room.

She immediately does her hair and makeup which takes her only twenty minutes. Her long blonde hair is bone straight and her eyes are an array of reds, false eyelashes, and gems. Red lipstick tops it off. She looks stunning.

She now moves on to me. She whips out some spray, and covers my hair with it, then grabs her hair curlers and begins to curl my hair. Huh. I have no idea what I look like with proper curls.

I let her work her magic then she proceeds to do my makeup. She begins on my eyes using eye shadow and puts on cat flicks. Duh. I'm a cat. She then swipes on a ton of mascara, a technique which will apparently make me look like a cat. She defines my cheekbones with bronzer then finishes with dark red lipstick. She instructs me to put my outfit on, which I do, as she puts hers on. We both strap on our headbands and face each other.

"You. Look. Hot!" we say to each other in unison then glance in the mirror. I am transformed. I do look like a cat. My eyes are slender, seductive and feline. My face looks mysterious. My lips look inviting and tempting. My hair is crazy, good crazy! Curls cascade down my back, the look making me appear dark and mysterious. I smile and launch myself into Amber's arms.

"Thank you!"

"Well, being an aspiring makeup artist, I could only dream of having someone as beautiful as you to practice on." She winks, then loops her arm through mine. "Then our shoes..."

"What shoes? I completely forgot!" I say in shock and horror. Amber chuckles.

"Don't worry, I picked some old ones of mine out for you." She hands them to me. They are red, thick-heeled and very high.

"You must be joking," I tell her. When I see her face, she's holding in a laugh.

"Loosen up. Those are mine." She laughs and puts a different pair into my hand. Stilettos. Not too high and elegant, just enough to add to my one night of being sexy and mysterious. I rush them on and stand up, admiring the look in the mirror. My legs have never looked so slim and . . . long.

Amber claps her hands together and squeals. "Kaidan is gonna go mad when he sees you!" she says a little too loudly.

"Shut up!" I tell her in a hushed voice. "He's just next door."

"Oh, who cares, best to let him know so he'll be prepared. Otherwise, he might just pounce on you." She winks. "Or it might just be the other way around, kitty cat."

"You're crazy." I tell her but she just laughs and pulls her shoes on.

"By the way, Jacob is gonna swing by to pick us up. He's going as Dracula. It's gonna be hilarious," she tells me, "and Pete . .

. who knows, he'll probably be something stereotypical like a zombie soccer player." She winks at me.

"Not this again." I grumble. "Pete is not into me."

"He has hots for you! Get it into your thick head!" Amber exclaims, playfully hitting me on the head.

"Ow!" I mock pain and rub where she hit me. She just rolls her eyes sassily.

"Anyway, we should head off." Her phone shrills and she answers it. "Hey Jake. Yup. Yeah. Cool. We'll be right out." She puts her phone in her pocket. "That was Jacob, he's waiting outside."

We go down the stairs where I see Will dressed as a werewolf, standing next to Kaidan who's in black jeans and a fitted black tee.

They look up as we walk down the stairs. Will's eyes are glued on Amber and as my gaze shifts, Kaidan's are on mine. I break eye to eye contact but even so, his eyes are still on me.

Neither say a word.

"We're off, Will. Have a nice time," I tell Will as I walk up to him. He looks over at me and snaps out of his trance.

"What the hell are you wearing? Go change!" he says. Amber saunters up to us and places her hand on his arm. He immediately looks over at her and his eyes turn into saucepans.

"I'll look after her, Will. I promise," she says seductively and Will is reduced into a pool of goo. He just stands there, stuttering.

"Okay and Kaidan, keep an eye on them," Will says, before moving out of the way to let us out. As Amber and I walk out the door, Jacob beeps us. We both laugh and slide into the car. Amber in the front and me—

"Gracie, you'll travel with me," Kaidan says. Jacob looks up at him and his eyes resemble Will's when he looked at Amber a moment ago.

"Um, no I won't. You can travel alone," I tell him, shuffling along the car seat. He opens the door and puts his hand on my wrist.

"Gracie. Get out of the car," he says in a low growl. For some reason I think he won't let this slip.

"Fine," I grumble. "See you guys at the party." And as I slide out of the car, I see Amber wiggle her eyebrows at me. I roll my eyes and step out, hearing Kaidan chuckle. Of course, he saw. Amber is about as subtle as an elephant in New York.

I fold my arms, refusing to put my seat belt on.

"Gracie, put your seatbelt on," he says, putting the key in the ignition. I ignore him.

"Gracie . . ."

"Are you hell-bent on making my life a misery?" I raise my eyebrows. "I'm the loser who has to have a babysitter. I don't need a lift there too. I wanted to travel with my friends, listening to music loud. I don't want to be with some psycho at a party for seventeen-year olds!"

Kaidan laughs, like properly laughs.

"You're hilarious, Gracie. I'll give you that," he says, cruising down the lane.

"Stop calling me Gracie."

"Put your seatbelt on," he says, glancing at me. I stick out my tongue and pull my seatbelt over me.

"God, you're like a child," Kaidan says, studying me once more.

"I'm nearly eighteen. Seventh of November," I tell him. He raises his eyebrows.

"Same as me," he says, and he almost sounds excited about it.

"You're turning twenty-one?!" I say in disbelief.

"Gracie, where did you get that from? I'm turning nineteen. I'm on my gap year," he explains.

"Oh, Mom said you were twenty. And what's a gap year?" I ask.

"The year in between high school and college. I'm working with your dad for experience. The money I earn goes to your dad, which means I can stay in your house having food and water provided for me."

"Oh. Cool," I say.

One whole year with Kaidan? You've got to be kidding me.

SEVENTEEN

When we arrive at the party, I feel my stomach fill with dread. Lucas is going to be here, drunk probably, and with a whole lot of anger towards me for standing him up. I take a deep breath and reach for the door handle.

"You don't have to go in if you don't want to, Gracie," Kaidan says slowly, noticing my obvious nerves. I shake my head at him.

"I'm fine. Let's go." With a surge of confidence, I open the door, spotting Amber and Jacob as they clamber out of the car in front of me. I rush over to them, mortified by the idea that people will see I have a babysitter with me.

"Grace! You can't leave him alone," Amber tells me as I catch up with them. I roll my eyes.

"Yes, I can. I don't need a babysitter." I fold my arms, before turning around to see if Kaidan has followed me. He hasn't but he is glaring at me. I turn back to my friends and they're giggling.

"What?" I ask them. They carry on sniggering so I raise my hand and swat at Jacob's arm. He frowns at me.

"Okay! It's just that . . . he's looking at you like he wants to rip all your clothes off." Jacob shrugs nonchalantly. He is unbelievable.

"He is not. That is the face of someone who wants to murder me in my sleep, not take my clothes off. Capiche?" I tell

91

them, feeling like I'm telling off two naughty children. They just wiggle their eyebrows at me.

"Whatever. I need a drink," I say, before grabbing their hands and marching into the party. The smell of alcohol and smoke hits me as soon as we walk in. The guy whose party it is (Martin, I think) has done an awesome job at decorating—he has pumpkins, cobwebs, spiders, and some Halloween drinks. We make a beeline for the drinks. Or so I try. I'm stopped by a hand on my wrist. I swivel around to see Kaidan glaring at me again.

"What's your problem?" I snap at him. He's receiving numerous approving looks from the girls in the room, causing a foreign feeling to swirl in my stomach.

"I am on strict orders by Will to look after you. So you can't just run off, okay?" he tells me. Now I feel like I'm the naughty child being told off. I throw my hands up in frustration.

"I just want to have fun with my friends! I'm not a baby, Kaidan," I tell him in annoyance. Before he can reply I power walk over to the drink table where Amber and Jacob are having a drinking competition.

"Okay, gross." Amber scrunches her nose. "I can't drink any more of that."

Jacob's arms go up in victory. "Winner winner!" he calls and I applaud him. Amber grabs a cup for me and places it into my hands.

"Pinch your nose when you drink it," she tells me. "I have no idea what they've put into that but it can't be good." I take a big sip and the acidic flavor in my mouth confirms that she's right. The drink is disgusting.

"Hey guys," comes the familiar voice of Pete. He greets Amber and Jacob by giving them a hug and I briefly wonder whether he's going to avoid me but he doesn't. He pulls me into a strong hug, filling my stomach with butterflies.

"How are you guys drinking that stuff?" Pete questions, eyeing our cups.

"It's the only drink here and we want to get drunk so . . ." Amber shrugs, taking another sip.

"Here, have some." Pete holds out a hip flask to Amber. Amber raises an eyebrow in suspicion, making Pete laugh. "It's vodka—cheap vodka, but better than that stuff." Amber takes a swig and passes it to Jacob. Jacob does the same and passes it to me.

"No." I hear from behind me. Oh, for the love of god. To spite him, I turn around, face him, lift the flask to my lips, and take a big sip. The spirit flows down my throat, scorching it as it goes. Then the distaste fades, giving me a warmth at the bottom of my stomach. Kaidan's face grows stormy.

"Are you trying to piss me off?" Kaidan shouts, walking closer to me. Pete immediately steps in between us.

"Woah, dude, calm down. It's just a bit of vodka." Pete takes the flask from my hand. "You're more than welcome to have some."

Kaidan narrows his eyes at Pete. "I'm fine." His eyes dart to me and he shakes his head. "I'll just wait for you in the car."

And before I can respond, he storms out of the room. I bite my lip awkwardly.

"Who is that?" Pete turns to me.

"It doesn't matter," I mutter, before taking the flask and gulping down some more vodka. Screw you, Kaidan.

*   *   *

I can't remember how much alcohol I've had. Amber is making out with Kyle (when did he even arrive?) and Jacob is nowhere to be seen. I'm playing beer pong with Pete and I'm losing.

Surprisingly, I haven't seen Lucas yet. But it's a big party and the night is young, so I'm sure I'll bump into him at some point.

"Score!" Pete calls as the ball drops in to my cup for the fourth time. I sadly look over at his triangle of cups, still in full formation. I suck at beer pong.

"Not again," I sulk, taking the ball from my cup and eyeing the brown liquid in it. I don't even like beer!

"I'll drink it," comes a voice behind me. I turn around to see Lucas leaning against the doorframe smugly. My stomach drops.

"It's all good," I slur. "I got it." I bring the cup to my lips and take a sip. The lukewarm liquid runs down my throat. "Okay." I put my hand up. "I haven't got it."

Lucas chuckles and makes his way over to the table. He takes the drink from my hand before finishing the whole drink in one gulp. "You're looking very sexy tonight, Grace," he tells me, taking the ball from the side of the table. Keeping his eyes on me, he throws the ball. My mouth drops open as it plops straight into one of Pete's cups. Pete's face is thunderous.

"Thanks," is the only word I say. Lucas shrugs and winks at me. I step back in shock. I thought he was mad at me?

"Alright, Alridge. Let's play," Lucas calls over to Pete, whose face is unmoving. He shakes his head.

"I was quite happy playing with Grace. Thanks," he calls back. Oh no.

"I am sure you were." He sniggers. "Winner of this game gets her for the rest of the night." My mouth drops open in disgust.

"Lucas, I am not a betting piece you can pass around!" I snap at him. Does he seriously think that I would do that?

"Done," comes Pete's voice. I look at him in shock. I thought he was a nice guy. I shake my head at him, before turning around and storming out of the room. I find myself in the dance floor, bodies hot and sweaty, couples pushed up against each other. Something (or someone) grabs my ass and I swivel around to see Jacob beaming at me. He winks, grabbing my hand and pulling me into him.

"I'm so drunk!" he shouts into my ear as if he's trying to perforate my ear drum.

"Me too!" I shout back with the same intensity. We move together with the music, thoughts of Lucas and Pete fading into the distance. As we dance, the room feels hotter and the music feels louder.

"I need air!" I tell Jacob, rushing off the dance floor and out of the room. As the cool air hits me, I feel nauseous. It's only a couple of seconds before I feel sickness creeping up my throat, proceeding to puke everywhere.

Then I feel hands on my hair, pulling it away from my face. My body convulses again, causing another wave of puke. The person holding my hair swears.

When my body is done emptying its insides, I turn to see who my knight in shining armor is. Tall, dark, and handsome greets me with a tilted head.

"Kaidan," I murmur. "Thanks."

"I think we should get you home." He places his arm around me, giving me support. Just in time, too, because my legs give way from underneath me.

"Jesus, Gracie. How much did you drink?" he asks, walking towards the car.

"Nothing!" I say quickly, before giggling. He sighs, muttering under his breath. We get to the car and Kaidan slowly helps me into the passenger seat.

"You're so grumpy," I tell him as he starts the car. "Do you hate me?" Kaidan shakes his head before pulling out onto the road.

"I don't hate you," he tells me, his eyes fixed on the road, "but I'm not here to make friends. I'm here for work."

"But you're nice to Will," I say, my words joining in a slur. Wow, really attractive, Grace. Kaidan sighs again.

"It doesn't matter," he mutters under his breath. In my drunken state, anger bubbles inside me and I release it by hitting Kaidan's arm.

"You're mean!" I say, before hitting him again. And again. And again. Kaidan stops the car in our driveway and looks over at me. Then the most unexpected thing happens.

Kaidan bursts out into laughter—full blown laughter, with-tears-from-the-eyes laughter. I frown in confusion, because from all the things I do, hitting him would be the last thing I would expect to make him laugh.

"You're funny, Gracie," he says through laughter. "I'll give you that."

EIGHTEEN

A hangover greets me in the morning. A head-pounding, stomach-spinning, sickness-inducing hangover. My first attempt at standing up results in a collapse back onto my bed.

"Ow," I murmur, rubbing my head as it pounds. I groan into my pillow while I mentally swear to never drink again. As I roll over, I see a glass of water and two pills on my bedside. *What the?!* I lean closer to see a note next to them.

Thank me later. – K

Through my pain I manage a smile. How thoughtful of him. And very, very unlike Kaidan. I slowly reach for the pills, popping them in my mouth and drinking the entire glass of water.

"Well, well, well," comes a voice from my door. I look over to see Will standing over me, looking smug.

"A little birdie told me that you got a little drunk last night." He chuckles. "Actually, I think the phrasing was 'Gracie was so drunk that she came back into the house, went into the bathroom, switched off the light, laid down, and said night night.'" He laughs again. "Sound about right?"

I groan into my pillow. Did I really do that? "Go away."

"You also apparently got into bed with all your clothes on." Will's eyes crease at the corners. I'm glad one of us is finding this funny. Horror sweeps through me though, as I realize I am wearing my pajamas. Did Kaidan get me changed?

97

"Don't worry," Will says, as if reading my thoughts. "You proceeded to strip all your clothes off and threw them at Kaidan's face, saying 'Do I look like a baby now?'" He gives me a stern look. Oh my god.

"You know, Will, I would have been totally fine without that information," I tell him, finally placing my feet on the ground and standing up.

"If you had come to my party then it wouldn't have happened," Will tells me in an I-told-you-so voice. "Stripping in front of someone you barely know isn't exactly appropriate behavior, Grace. And it's certainly not something I'm comfortable with. Next time you drink, you need to be more careful."

I narrow my eyes at him and push past him, murmuring "Whatever." I make my way down the stairs slowly and as I enter the kitchen, I see Dad and Kaidan working on some plans at the table.

"Morning, Grace," Dad says as I enter the room. "I heard that you were in a bit of a state last night." Has Kaidan told my entire family about my disgraceful state last night? I internally groan as I see the look on Dad's face.

"Dad, I can explain . . ." I begin, but he shakes his head.

"I'm not angry, darling. Of course, I want you to have fun. But drinking is a slippery slope. It can go terribly wrong. Next time, you need to be more sensible," he tells me in a serious voice.

I nod and turn my head to Kaidan angrily. I stare at him until he looks up from the plans.

"Morning," he mumbles, before turning his head back to his work.

Dad chuckles at my appearance before returning to his conversation with Kaidan. I narrow my eyes in distaste before making some eggs for breakfast.

"Do you want me to go get it?" Kaidan says as I catch the end of their conversation. Dad shakes his head and stands up.

"I'll get it." He walks out of the door in a rush. I frown at Kaidan in confusion.

"He left one of our plans at the office," Kaidan tells me bluntly. I nod in understanding as I stir my eggs. Then I slam the spoon on the side.

"Did you really need to tell my brother about last night?" I shout at him. He looks at me blankly.

"He asked what happened this morning, so I told him. I wasn't going to lie." He shrugs, keeping his eyes on his laptop. I sigh in frustration.

"You didn't need to tell him the explicit details!" I throw my arms up in frustration. God, he is insufferable!

"Like what, Gracie?" He looks at me sharply. "Explicit details like what, exactly? Like me waiting in the car for four hours to drive you home, or maybe it was the part where I held your hair back while you puked or maybe, just maybe, me buying you aspirin at six fricking a.m., so that you don't have a hangover," Kaidan yells at me, "because all of that sounds pretty accurate to me."

I step back, shocked at his words. He's right. For once, I agree with him. "Kaidan, I—" but he doesn't let me finish.

"Your eggs are burnt. And I'm trying to work, so take your hangover ass somewhere else," he snaps, returning to his computer screen once more. I look to my pan, where my eggs are cremated at the bottom of the pan. I rub my head in frustration and throw them in the trash.

"Thank you," I tell Kaidan as I leave the room. But his eyes don't even leave the screen.

*   *   *

Thank goodness it's a Saturday because I don't think I would have coped at school. I've thrown up twice, been through six pills, and I still feel on the edge of death. I hate hangovers.

I decide to take a walk, hoping that fresh air will be the cure to my hangover (setting my expectations high).

I've been walking for about fifteen minutes when I see it. I don't notice it immediately, because from a distance, it just looks like people talking. But when I get closer, I see it. Kyle is talking to a man wearing all black, and they look like they're having an argument. I stand behind a car so they can't see me and try to listen to what they're saying.

"That's not all of it," the man wearing black says to Kyle, clearly angry.

"I'm not lying to you, Dan. This week has been dry. Halloween was a bust," Kyle says apologetically. The guy wearing all black (his name is Dan, it seems) rubs his face angrily.

"Halloween is never a bust, Kyle." He growls. "It's the biggest drug night of the year." My stomach drops. Kyle is a drug dealer? Does Amber know?

"I'm telling you, man. No one was interested. Ask Lucas, he'll tell you himself," Kyle replies and my stomach sinks further. Is Lucas a drug dealer too? Was he on something on Halloween?

"I will," Dan snarls. "And if I find out you're lying to me, I'll come for you." He pushes Kyle backwards roughly. "I've done it before." Shivers run down my spine. *I've done it before.* What sort of guy is this?

"I don't doubt it." Kyle shrugs his jacket back onto his shoulders and paces away from Dan. Dan looks up and I can finally see his face; a long scar down the right side. My heart rate accelerates because there's a strange feeling in my stomach telling me I've seen that man before.

*   *   *

The man with the scarred face haunts my dreams. He chases me, calls after me, and threatens to kill me. My alarm blares through my nightmares and I wake up in a cold sweat.

"Just a dream." I breathe out and run my hands through my hair. The house is empty, apart from Will and I. Mom, Dad and Kaidan are all at work. I feel relieved because I still haven't faced Kaidan since he yelled at me yesterday.

"Woah, are you okay?" Will asks as I enter the kitchen. "You look like you've seen a ghost." I drag my feet over to the coffee machine. I feel as if I haven't slept at all.

"I had a bad night's sleep," I tell him, the image of the man with the scarred face haunting me. What was it about him that's haunting so much? Part of me wondered whether it was that I need to tell Amber that Kyle is getting involved with some dodgy people. But why does the scarred man keep reentering my mind?

"Looks like it," Will tells me. "I have soccer practice today and Mom is out. Are you going to be okay here by yourself?"

"Yeah sure," I tell him, but my voice shakes slightly as I say it. I call Amber immediately, asking her to come over. That man has really shaken me.

*   *   *

Amber arrives in a fluster.

"What's wrong?" I ask, my thoughts only focusing on Kyle and Dan. I need to tell her.

"Kyle," she says and my stomach drops. Does she know? "He's been acting so weird all week. I asked him about it this morning and he told me that if I brought it up again, he'd break up with me." She puts her face in her hands and lets out a sob.

"Amber . . ." I put my arm around her. I know exactly why he's been acting so strangely. "I have to tell you something." She looks up with panda eyes. I rub my finger under each eye to remove some mascara. She murmurs an apology. Deep breath. "Yesterday, I saw Kyle with a man. They were talking about drugs." I don't take any breaths between my words and it all seems to come out as one long word. But from Amber's reaction, I know she understood every single word.

"Kyle's dealing?" she asks and then swears. I place my hand on her back to comfort her. Wow, Kyle is a real asshole.

"And the guy, he was threatening him." I feel her tense up. "I'm worried about him, Amber." She lets out a sob and her body shudders.

"I have to break up with him, don't I?" she asks me weakly. I nod slowly. Because if Kyle is getting involved with those sorts of people, what sort of person does that make him?

"Everything was so perfect. He was so perfect. And now . . ." A tear falls down her cheek slowly. "Why do I always go for the wrong guys?"

"You didn't know," I tell her, and I really don't have any idea what else to say. She cries some more before looking up. Then she throws her arms around me. It shocks me for a second but I return the hug.

"I'm so glad I met you, Grace. You're awesome," she says, her voice thick with tears. "But whatever you do, please don't let Lucas sway you. He's the definition of the wrong guy." I nod. She doesn't need to tell me that. I know that for myself and his behavior at the Halloween party confirmed that for me.

"I know. He tried to use me as a betting wager last Friday," I tell her. Amber removes her arms from around me and frowns.

"What?"

"He and Pete agreed to play beer pong and whoever won got to spend the rest of the night with me." When the words come out of my mouth, they sound even more ridiculous than it felt at the time. Amber's mouth drops open.

"And who won?" Her tears have stopped. I smile at her, glad that I've managed to distract her.

"I didn't wait around to see the result, I was pissed off." I pause and giggle. "I also puked in front of Kaidan." A laugh bubbles out of Amber.

"I can't believe Pete did that." Amber runs her hand through her hair. "I thought he was one of the good ones." I nod in agreement. I thought so too.

"He definitely likes you, though."

"I thought that I liked him too but then he stooped to Lucas' level. So, I'm not really sure what I think anymore. And Kaidan..." I trail off, because I don't know how I feel about Kaidan. He infuriates me 99 percent of the time but maybe that infuriation is mistaken for something else.

"What about Kaidan?" Amber's eyes are wide. She always loves gossip.

"He looked after me on Halloween. His behavior is so unpredictable, I can't figure him out." I sigh, rubbing my face.

"I think he's sexually frustrated," Amber says statically. I burst out laughing, shocked by her comment. Kaidan is not sexually frustrated.

"Shut up." I hit her arm playfully. She just shrugs in a knowing way.

NINETEEN

Darkness, all I see is darkness. When my eyes crack open, I see a faint outline of a man lying on the floor of the alleyway. Men surround him, kicking him. They're hurting him. All I want to do is reach out and stop them, but I can't. I can't help him. So I scream.

"Leave him alone!" I scream, my voice hoarse. The men surrounding him turn to me. "Shut up, you little brat!" one yells and points a gun towards me. I then begin to scream. I scream and I—

"Gracie!" Kaidan's voice rings through my deep sleep. My eyes open suddenly to see Kaidan standing above me, shirtless. It takes me a second to realize that my face is wet.

"Are you okay?" he asks, his voice full of concern. I bring my hands to my face, wiping the tears off my cheeks.

"I'm fine," I manage, confusion lacing my tone. It was a nightmare. Just a nightmare. But it felt so real.

"You were screaming. It woke me up," Kaidan tells me bluntly. I rub my eyes, glancing at the clock. 3:05 a.m.

"Sorry." I wipe my face again, removing the remains of my tears. Kaidan's face softens slightly and sits down on the edge of my bed.

"Are you okay?" he asks me. "You don't normally scream in your sleep." I shrug.

"It's new to me too. I think I was having a nightmare." I shudder at the thought. The men, the gun, the screaming, it all seems familiar. Too familiar.

"You think?" he asks. I nod and sigh.

"It felt real. It really scared me." I pause. "You should go back to sleep, though." His eyebrows furrow and his eyes bore into mine. He looks like he's about to say something but instead, he stands up and leaves my room. As I'm greeted with silence, I realize the thumping sound of my heart in my chest.

*   *   *

I don't wake anyone else up by screaming for the rest of the night, which is good news. I do, however, have another dream about the man with the scarred face. I decide to have a cold shower to attempt to wash away the bad omens from last night. *They're just dreams, Grace.* I tell myself.

Will is the only one in the house again. Kaidan and Dad are working, and Mom is meeting a client. We make small talk while we eat breakfast, before driving to school.

As soon as we part ways at school, I hear someone come up behind me.

"Grace," says the voice, masculine and breathy. I turn around to see Pete, a frown on his face. I sigh and cross my arms, still feeling bitter about what happened at the party.

"Morning, Pete," I tell him bluntly. My lack of sleep last night is not helping my mood. He runs his hands through his hair.

"I am so sorry about Friday, Grace. I was drunk. I didn't know what I was doing," he apologizes. He does sound sincere.

"You shouldn't have agreed with Lucas, Pete." I shake my head. "You're so much better than him."

"I know. I was stupid," he says weakly. "Please just forget it happened. Please," he begs. I nod slowly, because I am not one to hold a grudge (except in Lucas Keith's case).

105

Today, we have to gather in the sports hall to receive some notices from the principal. Pete and I walk in together, immediately spotting Lucas on one of the far benches. He catches my eye and throws a wink in my direction. Ugh.

"Good morning, everyone. I hope you had a good weekend," Mr. Keith greets us. I yawn, zoning out as the principal reads out some notices. I begin to feel myself dozing off, but then loud music suddenly fills my ear drums. *What the?!* Mr. Keith looks as confused as me.

Is that . . . Justin Bieber?

"Oh my god," I hear Pete say next to me. I turn to see where his gaze is focused, seeing none other than Lucas Keith standing at the bottom of the bleachers, a microphone to his mouth.

"I know you love me I know you care," he sings, incredibly out of key. What on earth is he doing? Then I realize that not only are Lucas' eyes on me, but all of the school's as well. Is Lucas trying to serenade me? I immediately feel my face redden.

Lucas makes his way up the bleachers as he reaches the chorus. "Baby, baby, baby ooh!" he sings, getting closer to me. I frown at him, before noticing that the cheerleaders have begun to dance too. What is going on?

"I thought you'd always be mine." Lucas sits on the bench next to me and all I can do is stare at him with wide eyes. Then his hand is on mine, to guide me down the steps of the bleachers.

I want to bury myself in a hole.

He releases my hand and gestures to the cheerleaders who are in some elaborate formation, holding a large banner that reads *Grace, will you go to homecoming with me?*

Are you kidding me?

The song ends and all eyes are on me. I have now surpassed the color red and transcended into purple.

"So Grace, what do you say?" he asks, all grins. I frown at him some more, trying to figure out if this is a joke. But the grin on his face and the whole school in silence tells me that it's not. A voice in the back of my head reminds me that I should probably give him an answer. I bite my lip, pretending to consider his offer.

"I'm good, thanks."

The gymnasium is so quiet, you could hear an ant scuttle. I roll my lips into my mouth and swing my arms. Jeez. What a great way to start a Monday.

"Really?" Lucas says, breaking the silence. "After all of that?" I see his face has begun to redden too. I'm glad I'm not the only one humiliated by this. Then anger ignites in me.

"After all of what, exactly?" I ask him, but I don't wait for a response. "After you bullied me for my entire time at Jistie High? Is that what you're referring to?"

"Grace—" I don't let him even begin his sentence.

"And you think that because you do an elaborate display, I will miraculously forgive you?" I feel my voice begin to rise in volume. "Anyone can do that, Lucas. But you chose to be that idiot who was naïve enough to think it would work.

"So no, I won't go to homecoming with you. Not after that performance, not ever. You ruined my life, Lucas Keith, so the only thing I owe you is to return the favor," I yell. I don't wait around to see any reaction. I just turn around and storm out of the gymnasium.

TWENTY

I storm out of the school and into the car park. Screw attendance, I'm going home. I open my car door and climb into the passenger seat. It's then that I spot him, the man with the scarred face—he's sitting in the car next to me. My heart rate accelerates and the cogs in my brain begin to turn as a memory erupts from darkness.

His hand is cool in mine. "Did you enjoy the theatre, button?" he asks me. I swing our arms and nod my head quickly. We pass an alley way and voices begin to emerge.

"Look who it is," a man with a scar down his face jeers. "Where's my money, Jared?"

"Dan, please, I swear I will get it back to you!" Uncle Jared says, panic in his voice. The scarred man laughs, raising a black object in his hand.

"Wrong answer." And the gun goes off.

I come out from the flashback in a sweat. What was that? Heart rate high, I step on the accelerator and zoom out of the car park. I was right. There was a reason I recognized the man with the scarred face, Dan. But who is Uncle Jared, and why can't I remember him?

As I pull into my driveway, I question whether the flashback was real. It could have just been a figment of my imagination. But it felt so real. I rush into the house to find it as empty as I left it. Thank God. I really don't think I could deal with Kaidan's mood today.

Confusion eats away at me as I consider the flashback. Was it even a flashback? My mind could not have made that up. Unless I'm going crazy. But I'm not going crazy because Dan is real. Does that mean Uncle Jared is real? My mind reels continuously and my only resolution is to turn to Google. Not the most reliable of sources but it might help me all the same.

'Are flashbacks real?' I type into the browser.

A flashback, or involuntary recurrent memory, is a psychological phenomenon in which an individual has a sudden, usually powerful, re-experiencing of a past experience or elements of a past experience, Wikipedia reads. A past experience. That means it could have happened but then why can't I remember it?

My mind immediately flashes to my grandfather, who was diagnosed with dementia when I was six. I barely remember him and my parents never let me visit him in his care home. They always told me that he was aggressive and he had no idea who I was.

But I can't have dementia. You're brought up to believe that dementia is something that manifests itself when you're older—hardly something you have to trouble yourself with when you're only seventeen. So, I decide to google *forms of memory loss.* My heart leaps in my chest as the first link pops up. I click on it and begin to read the article. It lists several forms of amnesia, such as retrograde, anterograde, transient global, and a couple of others that don't apply to me. Then my stomach drops as I reach the last one.

Dissociative amnesia:
Severe trauma or stress can also cause dissociative amnesia. With this condition, your mind rejects thoughts, feelings, or information that you're too overwhelmed to handle.

Trauma. Trauma like seeing someone being shot like in the flashback. It seems far-fetched, but a feeling of dread is pooling in my stomach, telling me that I could be right. I feel my eyes beginning to fill with tears and suddenly they're cascading down my face and sobs are racking through my body. How could this have happened? And if it did happen, then have my parents been keeping it from me? Have I been lied to my entire life?

The sound of the door shutting brings me back to the present. I need to talk to my parents because if they have been lying to me, then they have some serious explaining to do.

I wipe the tears and rush downstairs to see Kaidan and Dad in the kitchen. Dad gives me a smile and Kaidan doesn't even register my presence.

"Have you been crying, Grace? Your eyes look red," Dad asks me in a concerned voice. I sniff and fold my arms.

"Who is Uncle Jared, Dad?" The words come out of my mouth so quickly I can't stop them. But as I see his face whiten, I realize I was right to have my doubts. I'm not going crazy.

"What do you mean?" Dad tries to play the fool. Kaidan looks between us, finally acknowledging my presence.

"You know exactly what I mean." I'm being overconfident in the hope that he won't lie to me. I could be wrong and this could all be a figment of my imagination, but the look on Dad's face tells me that it's not.

"I should leave," Kaidan says awkwardly, sensing the tension in the room. He begins to leave, but I put my arm across the door.

"No, you're staying. I want you to witness this so he can't lie," I tell him, my voice fiery. Kaidan looks to Dad who just shakes his head. I narrow my eyes at him.

"Kiddo, everything I do in life is because I love you," he begins, and I roll my eyes. 'I love you' is not a get-out-of-jail-free card, Dad.

"Just tell me. Tell me who Jared is," I demand. Dad exhales, his face now ashy.

"Jared was my brother." And those four words make my life turn upside down. Memories of strolling in the park, going to the movies, eating ice cream rush into my brain like a tsunami. Uncle Jared.

"Why don't I remember him?" Tears form in my eyes once again. Dad's eyes soften and he attempts to put his hand on mine but I swat it away.

"Grace, now is really not the time—"

I cut him off. "Why don't I remember him?" I shout, tears trickling down my cheeks now. How dare he lie to me.

"Jared was shot after he took you to see your favorite play. You watched him die." Dad's voice is croaky and I can see tears forming in his eyes too. My flashback, the one with Dan, the scarred man. It was real.

"I remember," I manage, before breaking down into a sob, "I saw him." I let the tears fall down my face because memories of Jared are slowly slotting into place. He was my best friend.

"You saw him?" Dad asks, his voice breaking. I shake my head.

"I saw the shooter. He was at my school," I tell him and Dad's face drops.

"Why on earth was he at a high school?" Dad asks, anger in his voice. I shrug, before wiping away my tears.

"I really have no idea."

*   *   *

I'm going to see a doctor. Dad didn't want me to because he's worried about me breaking down again. But I need to know why I forgot those memories of Jared.

111

I pack my handbag in my room and I'm interrupted by a knock on the door. I tell whoever it is to come in, only to see Kaidan with a solemn look on his face.

"Not now, Kaidan," I huff, feeling too drained to deal with his mood today. He cocks his head to one side.

"Rob wants me to accompany you to the psychiatrist since you refuse to go with him," he tells me formally as if he's been scripted.

"I'm fine by myself," I tell him, swinging my backpack over my shoulder. Kaidan places his arm in front of me to block the doorway.

"You don't have a choice. I'm coming," he tells me, his voice monotone. I sigh and roll my eyes.

"Whatever." I storm past him, make my way down the stairs and out of the house. I climb into the passenger seat, Kaidan shortly behind me. We drive in silence, and for the life of me I can't figure out what he's thinking. His face is stony, but I can detect a glimmer of warmth in his eyes.

I think he cares about me.

We pull into the hospital and I feel my heart leap in my chest. I am about to find out what is wrong with me. I really hope I'm not crazy.

Once we're in the waiting room, it seems like hours before the nurse calls out my name. My stomach drops and I gulp. Here we go. I stand up, saying bye to Kaidan before following the nurse down a corridor and into a room.

"Afternoon, Grace." The doctor stands up and shakes my hand. "I'm Doctor Kingston."

"Hi." I sit on the chair and link my hands together, rubbing my palms anxiously. "I, um, I think I have some sort of amnesia," I say, unsure of how to phrase it. I bet they get all sorts of cases of people diagnosing themselves with diseases off google.

"Have you been having problems with your memory?" he asks me seriously. I exhale and nod.

"I recently have been remembering things from when I was younger. Six, I think. Around the time of my uncle's death," I tell him and he manages to keep his face straight.

"I see. How many memories have returned?" he asks.

"I forgot that my uncle even existed. It's as if my memory completely wiped him out after he died," I say, my voice shaky.

He nods and gives me a small smile.

"Okay, Grace. Are there any other more recent cases of memory loss?" he asks me and I shake my head.

He nods, and turns to his computer before pulling up a document.

"Your medical history does not indicate any head injuries around the time of the memory loss, nor brain diseases," he tells me frowning. "And I assume you were not intoxicated when you were six," he jokes, clearly attempting to lighten the mood.

I shake my head and chuckle.

"Okay, Grace. Your memory loss is not associated with brain injury, which is good. I'm going to run an MRI to check if your brain is looking normal," he tells me, giving me a warm smile. I let out a shaky breath. He tells me to follow him and so I do.

The next couple of hours blur together as I'm wheeled from one room to the next, into a strange room with a white dome. Doctors place me in the machine for some time before wheeling me back to the original room.

Doctor Kingston returns to the room. "Good news, Grace. The CT revealed that your brain is normal. I am going to refer you to our resident psychiatrist who will perform an examination on you," he tells me. I frown.

"Is that it? Can't you just tell me what's wrong with me?" I ask him, feeling anger and frustration. All of those elaborate measures and exposing my brain to radiation just for him to tell me that my brain is normal?

"There is nothing medically wrong with you, Grace. And believe it or not, that is a good thing." He places his clipboard down on the table and passes me a piece of paper. "The psychiatric wing can be found by taking the elevator to the third floor and just follow the signs. I've paged Doctor Hanson, our resident psychiatrist. He'll be waiting for you." I sigh and take the paper from his hand, before walking out of the room.

Kaidan stands up when he sees me, looking at me with questioning eyes.

"We're going to the psychiatric wing," I tell him.

"Did the doctor tell you what's wrong?" he asks me with concern in his voice. I shake my head.

"Apparently there's nothing wrong with me medically speaking. Just crazy." I put my finger to my temple and circle it. Kaidan chuckles.

"You're not crazy, Gracie," he tells me but I just shake my head because I am.

TWENTY-ONE

"Miss Connely?" A man pokes his head into the waiting room. He is dark skinned, with a very short cut of white hair. He is 60, 65 at most. I stand up in response. This must be Doctor Hanson.

"Hi," I tell him and he gives me a warm smile. I immediately feel comfortable with him.

"Doctor Kingston sent up your information. Memory loss after traumatic stress?" he checks with me. I nod.

"Okay, Grace. I am going to ask you some sensitive questions, okay? Let me know if you are feeling unwell or uncomfortable at any time, and we can stop," he tells me.

"Okay."

Doctor Hanson asks me a range of questions about my thoughts and feelings regarding the incident. They all seem to blur into one and I get the gist of what he's trying to get at—are you a mental patient?

"You have a condition called dissociative amnesia, Grace." Dr. Hanson eventually tells me. "It's localized, which means you're only unable to remember few events—events involving your uncle. This type of amnesia is extremely common after traumatic or stressful life events," he explains.

"So, I'm crazy?" I ask with a slight laugh in my voice. The doctor shakes his head.

"Definitely not. Childhood trauma is a key predisposition for dissociative amnesia. A lot of people don't get their memory back, so you are a very lucky and a very rare case," he tells me and I nod. He's right, I should be grateful.

"I am going to schedule an appointment for once a week so we can monitor your progress. With the help of several sessions, I'd like to think that all of the missing memories may return." He gives me a gentle smile. I thank him and leave the room.

Dissociative amnesia.

I spot Kaidan sitting in a chair waiting for me, head in hands.

"Kaidan," I manage, and then my eyes fill with tears again.

"Gracie?" He stands up and I fall into his chest, wrapping my arms tightly around him. He's tense at first but eventually caves and wraps his arms around me.

"It's going to be okay, Gracie," he says into my hair. "Let's go home."

"Kaidan, I'm sorry about the party," I say as I pull away from the hug. His expression turns stormy.

"Let's just go home," he repeats, his voice monotone once again. I frown, a single tear falling down my cheek.

"I was just apologizing," I say, slightly stung. "There's nothing wrong with that." He turns around and walks towards the elevator. I follow him, grabbing his arm.

"Don't just ignore me, Kaidan," I snap at him, sadness turning into anger. He silently presses the button and watches the doors close. I narrow my eyes. I don't want to have a screaming match in the middle of a hospital, so I stay silent, while anger bubbles inside of me.

"Kaidan, you can't ignore me now," I say once we're in the parking lot.

"There's nothing to discuss, Grace," he snaps. "You were a mess, I took care of you. It's no big deal. Let's just go home."

"Why? Why are you in such a rush?" I snap back.

116

"Because I said so!" His voice raises and I flinch. He walks in a circle and sighs before stopping in front of me.

"You don't need to shout," I say feebly and push past him, stomping towards the car. I slide into the front seat and slam the door with as much power as I can. I watch him as he rubs his face, contortion all over it. He then proceeds to angrily open the driver's door and slam it with more force than I did.

In all honesty, I'm expecting an apology. But Kaidan doesn't say anything, he just starts the car and pulls out of the space quickly.

I spare him a quick glance and he still has that stony expression on his face. "Why are you so mad?"

"Jesus Gracie, can you please just stop talking for five minutes?" he raises his voice. I flinch yet again and fold my arms over my chest.

"I have a mental disorder and all you can do is yell at me!" The tears cascade down my cheeks, letting him see me cry.

I wipe my cheeks and stare out of the window, where the weather takes a turn for the worst. Rain begins to pour and we are plummeted into silence. Kaidan pulls over on the side of the road.

"What do you want me to say? Huh?" he shouts. "Poor Grace, everything is about Grace. Take a reality check, not everything is about you."

"Wow." I cast him one look before stepping out of the car and into the pouring rain. I start walking. My shoes already beginning to soak through.

After I have walked several yards, I hear Kaidan's door slam shut, followed by running footsteps behind me.

"Grace!" he yells, grabbing me at the waist. I swivel around to face him and he already has raindrops dripping down his face. It's hard to distinguish my tears from the rain.

"What, Kaidan?" I shout back with all my might. He stares at me for a good 10 seconds before slowly taking a step away.

"You'll catch a chill out here. Get back in the car," he says quietly. I push a strand of wet hair from my face.

"I'll walk home," I wrap my arms around my stomach, a habit I picked up from my fat days. I turn away from him and start walking away.

"You don't always have to be so damn stubborn," he mutters, but I hear him loud and clear. I turn to face him again.

"You know what? I think I'm allowed to! I've had one of the worst days in my life and you're making a big deal because apparently I think everything is about me?" I'm yelling now. "Surprisingly, the day you get diagnosed with amnesia tends to be one where it is, in fact, all about me. And to think I thought you had managed to somehow change your personality from being a rude, unfriendly bastard to being slightly tolerable. Guess I was proved wrong, huh." My voice drops down a bit and I realize I'm panting.

Kaidan runs his hands through his hair. "I didn't ask for this." His eyes go back to that cold ice that I thought I'd forgotten.

"I'm sorry?" I snap at him. He narrows his eyes.

"I said I didn't ask for this. I didn't ask for my gap year to be spent with some teenage girl who thinks the world revolves around her. I didn't ask to be landed with being a babysitter for someone who can't remember a couple of things. I didn't ask for you, Grace." His voice is low and I feel tears gathering in my eyes again. "So, if you wish, walk home. I won't stop you." And with that, I watch him as he storms back to his car and drives off, leaving me on the pavement.

Cold. Wet. Miserable.

I let the rain fall on me. I let the tears run down my cheeks as my mind goes over and over his harsh words. A sob racks through my body and I crouch down onto the pavement. My legs collapse from underneath me and I begin to sob and sob.

Just when I thought that Kaidan could have changed for the better. He seemed like a completely different person. I should have known it was all an act.

I don't know how long I've been lying there, but when a car pulls up beside me, I'm pretty sure my lips are blue. I'm so cold that I'm moving in and out of consciousness. A small glimmer of hope runs through me, hoping Kaidan has come back to get me.

"I can't go home . . ." I mumble. "Don't make me . . . I don't want to see him . . ."

But I don't know if it's Kaidan because by the time the arms envelope me, I'm gone.

TWENTY-TWO

When I wake up, I'm surrounded by unfamiliar grey walls. Itchy cotton sheets are tangled around me. The first thing I notice is my clothing. I am no longer in my wet clothes. I am in a soft shirt. I look around at my surroundings. I'm in a small room with a wooden chair in the corner and a bedside table next to me. I see a picture on the table and squint my eyes in order to distinguish the person who saved me from the rain.

Dark eyebrows, dark hair. Pete.

I climb out of bed slowly, aches running all through me. 2:04 p.m. the clock reads. I sit on the edge of the bed and drink some water.

"You're awake," I hear a voice come from the door and I look over to see Pete standing in the doorway with two mugs in hand. I frown at him, confused about how I got here.

"First things first," he says while placing the mugs down onto the desk. "I didn't undress you. Amber did."

"Amber?" I frown, completely confused. He nods.

"Amber and I were on the way to the gym for her shift and we saw you sitting on the curb." His eyes soften. I chuckle.

"I had an argument with Kaidan," I explain, but it's really not that funny. Anger ignites in me when I think of what he did.

"What a prick," Pete says bluntly. "I can't believe he left you in the rain like that." I shrug because he's right. Kaidan is a prick.

"Amber had to leave for her shift after she got you changed," Pete continues. "So we decided to put you to bed here, to get warm."

"Thank you," I say, because I'm lucky I didn't get pneumonia. He smiles.

"I brought you cocoa." He passes me a mug which smells deliciously like chocolate. I take it eagerly and have a sip. *Mmm.*

"Thanks again," I say, giving him a smile. He nods.

"So last time I saw you was when Lucas did that elaborate performance." Pete laughs. "You were awesome, by the way. Totally awesome." I laugh with him.

"Thanks. I was so embarrassed," I tell him.

"You shouldn't have been. After you left, the principal took Lucas away from the gymnasium. Rumor has it, he's been in detention every day since it happened," Pete says and my mouth drops open.

"Punished by his own uncle? Jeez, that's harsh." I laugh, and Pete laughs with me.

"I know, um, that you said no to Lucas," Pete begins after our laughter has subsided. "But I would love it if you came to homecoming with me."

Boom. Butterflies.

"Really?" is the only word that comes from my mouth. His lips tilt to one side in a half smile.

"Yeah." He shrugs. "You're pretty darn awesome."

I smile. "Why not? It'll be fun," I tell him as butterflies fly around my stomach manically. He raises his eyebrows.

"Is that a yes, then?" he asks.

I nod. "Yes. It's a yes, Pete."

*   *   *

Pete drives me home and I try to sneak back into my room without anyone noticing me in his shirt.

121

"Gracie?" I hear that oh-so-familiar Australian accent. "I am so sorry—"

He comes into my room and cuts off what he was saying. "Whose shirt is that?"

"Pete's," I say bluntly, placing my other clothes on my bed.

"Pete? What were you doing with him?" He folds his arms. I ignore him and fold my clothes in silence.

"And why exactly are you wearing his shirt?" he asks, anger clipping his tone. I stay silent again. I don't want to give him the satisfaction of making me angry.

"Answer me," he demands. When I remain silent, he makes this noise that sounds very similar to a growl. "Grace." When he doesn't call me Gracie, I know he's getting angry.

"Because I nearly froze to death out in the rain, I needed dry clothes to wear," I say, turning around to glare at him. He narrows his eyes at me.

"You were the stubborn one. You put that on yourself. You got out of the car," he says angrily.

"And you were the one who made sure I stayed out," I snap, before regaining my calm. "Get out of my room, Kaidan."

He shakes his head and storms out of the room slamming his door shut, probably trying to make a point. I sigh and run my hands through my hair, before shutting my door and taking Pete's shirt off. My phone buzzes and I'm quick to check it.

Homecoming dress shopping. Today. Be there or be square.
    A x

The text from Amber reads. I chuckle. Nothing like a bit of retail therapy to get my mind off Kaidan and my amnesia.

*　　*　　*

I meet my two best friends at the mall, having a huge reunion hug even though we've only been apart for a day and a half.

"So, guess who asked me to homecoming," I tell them, feeling giddy. Amber and Jacob look at each other knowingly.

"You knew?" I ask them and they burst into laughter.

"He was going to do something more elaborate but after Lucas' epic failure, he thought he should go minimalistic. And it worked!" Amber says.

"We're going together," Jacob says, linking his arm into Ambers. "Because men are trash, honey." He clicks his fingers. "Except for Javi."

We wander around the shops for hours, Jacob deciding on an elaborate flower tux and Amber settling on a golden silk dress. She looks stunning in it. I, however, cannot find anything that suits me.

"Amber, I'm just going to have to settle for something." I sigh, running my hands through my hair.

"No," she snaps. "You are going to look drop dead gorgeous. Now let's go and get you an amazing dress."

So, we go into yet another store and as I look around at the mediocre dresses, I begin to lose hope.

"I found it!" I suddenly hear Jacob cheer. I spin around to see him holding a beautiful strappy red dress, floor length, with red buttons leading all the way up the back. I grin and leap over to him, taking the dress from his hands.

"You're an angel. Do you know that?" I ask, pinching his cheeks.

"Get your beautiful ass into the fitting room, young lady," he says. So I rush into the changing room to put the dress on. A pair of black suede heels with an open toe are passed underneath the door.

"I think these would go nicely," Amber pipes, and I hear them giggling together outside. I pull the silky fabric over me and slip my feet into the gorgeous heels. I glance in the mirror and lose my breath. The dress is simple yet beautiful and sophisticated. The heels give me amazing height, making me seem tall and elegant. I open the door to Amber's and Jacob's awaiting faces and their faces drop.

"What? Is it bad?" I question, thinking my judgment of how I look is wrong. They're shaking their heads immediately.

"You look amazing. Pete's going to go mental," Jacob says, eyeing me up and down.

"Red is his favorite color as well," Amber says seductively and winks. I shake my head and sigh.

"So, I'll get these then?" I conclude and they nod their heads eagerly. I grin and return to the dressing room before paying for the dress and returning home.

TWENTY-THREE

As I walk through the front door of my house, I know something is up. Mom, Dad and Will are all sitting at the kitchen table. Kaidan is nowhere to be seen. That means one thing and one thing only—a family meeting.

"Grace, can you please join us?" Dad tells me, gesturing to the seat opposite him. I want to tell him no, because he and Mom have been lying to me for most of my life. But I know that this will be about Jared.

"I'm hoping you've been brought up to speed," I tell Mom and Will bluntly. "I remember Jared which means I know what lying assholes you are." It comes out as rudely as I meant it. Can you blame me? I have been living with dissociative amnesia my entire life.

"Language, Grace," Mom says instinctively. "I know you're angry, but I think you need to hear your father out."

I sigh. "I have one question for you Mom," I say. "Did you know that I lost my memory?"

"Yes, but Grace—"

"And you didn't take me to a doctor," I say. "That's pretty bad parenting. Don't you think?" Her face turns beets red and she goes quiet. I know I'm being harsh but I can't help it.

"You are being rude, Grace," Dad speaks up. "I think if you remembered everything, you'd be glad that those memories were gone."

I narrow my eyes at him. "I'm sure that's the case. But you should have got me checked. I could have had something wrong with my brain."

"We knew that your brain was fine," Dad blurts, and immediately looks like he regrets it.

I cock my head to one side. "What?"

He sighs before saying, "Dissociative amnesia is genetic."

"I don't follow," I say, darting my eyes to Will, whose eyes are firmly on the counter. He's avoiding eye contact with me.

"Dissociative amnesia tends to run in families, Grace. And as you know, it is caused by a stressful event," Dad continues and I still don't follow him. Neither of my parents have it as far as I'm aware. Then it clicks. I thought Granddad had dementia, but maybe he had it too.

"But Granddad had dementia," I say, the cogs slotting into place. "Right?"

Both my parents shake their heads. "He didn't. You and Will were too young to know what dementia was, let alone dissociative amnesia," Dad says carefully.

I look at Will whose eyes are now on me. "I didn't know either, Grace. They told me last year," Will says. "They told me that Jared had moved to Australia when it happened. And that it was a secret."

"Why lie?" I turn my attention back to my parents.

"Murder is not something that you can explain to children aged six and eight, Grace," Dad says bluntly. "We made the decision to not tell you both, because it would have severely impacted you."

"And Granddad? Why lie about him too?" I ask. My parents look at each other tentatively and Mom nods.

"He developed dissociative amnesia following Jared's death, too. His, however, was more immediate. The day after, he was asking after Jared. He was living in the past," Dad explains. "I couldn't bear to tell him that Jared was dead.

126

"After a psychiatrist diagnosed him, he engaged in therapy at his care home. Slowly but surely, his memories returned." Dad rubs his face in distress. "But that's when your memory began to disintegrate, Grace. And we knew the symptoms. We knew you had it, too."

"So, you decided that I could never see my grandfather again?" I ask, confusion flooding through me.

"We were worried that you would be a trigger for him," Dad says with his eyes closed. "His amnesia is a little severe than yours. Anything relating to Jared would instantly affect his memories."

Then realization sets in. I understand why they did it. I do. "I forgive you."

All three of them look shocked. "Really?" Dad's voice breaks.

"Yes. I understand what you did. But I do have one condition," I say.

"Of course," Dad says eagerly. I take a deep breath.

"I would like to see Granddad."

No one says anything for a couple of moments. Mom is the first to break the silence.

"Grace, you heard what your father just said, didn't you?" she says it carefully as if I'm a mental patient (but who am I kidding, I basically am one, right?).

"I did. But I want to see him. He is the only person who knows what I'm going through," I say, folding my arms.

"Grace—" Mom begins but Will cuts her off.

"Let her go, Mom. She needs it." He gives me a warm smile. Best brother in the world I think. Dad nods in agreement.

"I'll come with you," he says. "I think it would help you both."

*   *   *

127

Nerves bubble inside me as we pull into the parking lot of the care home. Dad reaches for my hand and gives it a squeeze. I nod at him, and we proceed to make our way inside. The elevator seems to take forever. My nerves are squirming inside my stomach like wiggling snakes. The elevator dings and we step out. This is it.

"Ready, Grace?" Dad asks and I nod. We step into the room and in the chair sits an old man with white hair. As I step closer, recognition seeps through me and just like that, another foreign memory reappears.

They're talking in low voices. I look down at my flashing trainers, leading up to my patterned grey tights. Mommy insisted I wore a dress. She's never been pleased about my want to wear trousers everywhere. I guess having a fashion-obsessed mother means I have to dress well too. Dad talks to Uncle Jared lowly.

"Jared, you're a grown man now. You can't be childish like this."

"It wasn't even that much money, Rob." Uncle Jared combs his fingers through his hair.

"Borrowing money from a gang isn't a good idea, Jared. No matter the amount," Dad says. He quickly looks over to me and sees me looking.

"Grace, you shouldn't listen into people's conversations. It's rude."

"Sorry, Daddy."

I blink out of my flashback and look to my grandfather. He gives me a smile. I try to smile back but my mind is reeling from the memory. Jared borrowed money from a gang? Is that why he was killed? I take a deep breath and try to act normally.

"It's been a while," I muster to say. At first, I'm answered with silence. Then Granddad bursts into a course laugh. Dad starts to chuckle which eventually makes me join in. With a big smile on my face, I walk over to Granddad's chair and wrap my arms around his shoulders.

"It's good to see you," I tell him.

128

"You too, Grace." He gestures to the seat next to him. "I take it from your visit that your father has finally told you about Jared?"

Dad steps forward. "Pops, be careful."

Granddad swishes his hand at his son and gives a hearty laugh. "It's been twelve years, Rob. I think my memories will be okay. Now, do your old man a favor and grab me a coffee," Granddad says. Dad rolls his eyes and reluctantly leaves the room.

Granddad turns his attention back to me. "Where were we?"

"Jared. I just got diagnosed with dissociative amnesia," I tell him and he nods.

"It's a little bitch, isn't it?" Granddad says, laughing.

I smile and nod. "It really is, though, my psychiatrist says I should regain most of my memories with therapy. My psychiatrist says I should regain all my memories with therapy," I explain.

"Mine are mostly there. Sometimes, I have spells where I believe that Jared is alive. And those times are like gold dust to me. It means I get to be with my boy again." He shrugs and takes my hand. "You are just like him, you know. Ballsy and determined."

I smile and feel my eyes water. "I wish he was here to explain to me, explain why it happened," I say and when I see the look on Granddad's face, I realize I have made a grave mistake.

"It wasn't my fault, Rob," he says, his face stony. Tears gather in his eyes and he grasps my hand tightly. "I didn't do it."

"Granddad, it's me, Grace," I say, panic-stricken. Granddad isn't even looking at me now, his eyes are distant and empty.

"It was Dan. It wasn't me!" He begins to sob. "I didn't kill him. I didn't kill Jared!"

TWENTY-FOUR

"What happened?" Dad reenters the room swiftly. I move away from Granddad, who is murmuring under his voice. I run my hands through my hair.

"I don't know! We were talking about Jared and he just flipped!" I cry, staring at my grandfather in disbelief. Dad sits opposite him and takes his hand, before whispering to him words I can't hear.

Granddad begins to calm down, taking deep breaths. His tears stop, and his eyes turn to me. "Grace, I'm so sorry," he says, a single tear dripping down his cheek. "It's been years since that happened."

"I knew I was right to be worried," Dad says angrily. "You said it would be fine, Pops."

"Last time was so long ago. I thought I was fine," Granddad replies, pain in his voice. "My memories are fine, Rob. It's just a blip."

"It's not fine. You should have been more responsible. For all you knew, Grace could have had a fit too!" he yells.

"She's not as bad as me. You know that," Granddad replies. I'm lost in confusion. My mind fixated on Granddad's words. *I didn't kill him, I didn't kill Jared!* I know it was the scarred man, Dan, who killed Jared, and from his earlier words, Granddad knows that too.

So why did he say that?

*   *   *

Dad and I return home after the nurses took over the care of Granddad. My visits have to be short but often according to the resident psychiatrist. He told me I carry too many weighted memories.

I can't help but think that Dad is still hiding something. Granddad's words are haunting me, and I think he was more involved in Jared's death than I've been led to believe.

But for now, I decide to leave it to rest because homecoming is tomorrow and I believe it's time for me to have some normalcy in my life.

As I walk down the corridor and into my room, I see that Kaidan's door is open, and he's working on his laptop on his desk. We still haven't properly spoken after the curb incident and I am in no mood to speak to him today.

I glance at my dress hanging by my wardrobe, reminding me that Pete is taking me to homecoming tomorrow. Butterflies swoop in my stomach and I feel giddy! My phone buzzes and I check it.

Javi is doing our hair tomorrow for free!! 2 p.m., then we'll get ready at yours? A x

The text from Amber reads. I reply telling her that that works for me, before falling onto my bed. Wow. What an exhausting day. I close my eyes to take a nap, and it's barely been ten seconds before I hear a rap on my door.

"What?" I groan, before turning my head to see Kaidan at the door. I close my eyes. "Go away, Kaidan."

"I was just going to ask how you're doing. After the whole amnesia thing," he says, his tone awkward. My eyes snap open and I sit upright.

131

"Fine, no thanks to you," I snap, folding my arms across my chest.

"Gracie, I know I was out of line, okay?" His eyebrows furrow and he steps into my room. "I came to apologize."

I blink in surprise. Kaidan apologizing? Surely not. "Is this a joke?" I ask, and he shakes his head.

"I shouldn't have been such a dick. I was wrong," he says, and I can barely believe my ears. Never in my life have I thought Kaidan would apologize to me.

"Well, today is a day of forgiving, apparently," I tell him, shrugging. "So, we're good."

"Good," Kaidan says but remains hovering at my door. I raise an eyebrow at him.

"You can go now," I say, before lying back down onto my bed.

"Gracie, you sound pissed," he says, before sitting on the bed next to me. I groan and sit up again.

"No, I just want to take a nap," I tell him. "I've had an exhausting day."

He sighs and looks into my eyes. "You're my boss' daughter," he tells me.

I frown at him, confused. Yeah, I know that. I may have amnesia, but I haven't forgotten that little detail. "Your point is?" I question.

"Your dad is employing me. So, naturally, that makes our relationship tricky. That's why I get so angry when I have to look after you. I'm not here to babysit. I'm here for work experience," he says, and I furrow my eyebrows.

"Okay, are you apologizing or not? Because you just called me a baby, again," I snap, frustrated. Doesn't he know how to apologize like a normal person? Probably not.

"I am. I just wanted to explain. And I don't think you're a baby," he tells me seriously.

"Good to know." I laugh, and before I know it, I'm laughing so hard that my stomach hurts. Kaidan looks at me like I'm crazy.

"You're weird," he says, a slight smile making his way onto his lips. I grin.

"So are you, Kanye." I wink at him, before continuing to laugh. Kaidan rolls his eyes and a smile finally makes its way onto his face.

"I swear to god, Gracie," he chuckles.

"I knew I'd get to you eventually." I smile at him, and we fall into silence. He stares at me deeply and my stomach begins to feel funny. But not in the way it does when I think of Pete, no. When I'm with Kaidan, my entire world stops. I forget about everything—Jared, Granddad, the scarred man. They all go away. It's just me and him.

TWENTY-FIVE

Beep. Beep. Beep.

"Shut up!" I yell at my alarm as if it's a person. Of course, it doesn't stop. It just continues to beep until I slam my hand down on it. I groan and sit up, glancing at my phone. 8 a.m. on a Saturday.

Morning! We have a tight schedule! Get ur ass outta bed!!
Love u, A x

The text from Amber reads. I trust Amber to have the homecoming day planned down to each minute. I drag my body from bed and stretch out my aching muscles. Despite only going to the gym a couple of times a week now, my body still isn't used to the constant exercise.

I wander downstairs to see Kaidan and Will eating breakfast at the table.

"Morning. Want some?" Will mumbles through a mouthful of pancake. The maple aroma drifts into my nose and I almost succumb to temptation.

"Nope," I tell him as I open the fridge and grab the eggs. "It's homecoming, and I need to fit into my dress." Will mutters something under his breath. I raise an eyebrow at him.

"Something to say, Will?" I blink my eyelashes at him. He rolls his eyes at me and flicks his hand, as if to say nothing. Sure, Will, sure.

"So, who's your date to homecoming then?" Will asks me. Ever since he's graduated high school, I feel as if he wants to live vicariously through me. He's taking a year out before college and his life purely consists of college applications and soccer. Sometimes, he does house parties.

"None of your business," I tell him nonchalantly, stirring my eggs in the pan. Will stands up and frowns at me.

"Wait, you're actually going with someone?" he asks, looking concerned. Ouch.

"How nice of you to speak so highly of me, brother," I say sarcastically. Will leans beside the cooker to make eye contact with me.

"It's not . . . Lucas, is it?" Will asks with anger in his tone.

I laugh at the thought. "Of course not, Will," I tell him. "I'm going with Pete." I wait for his reaction in suspense. Instead of yelling, shouting or telling me that boys my age are immature, he simply nods.

"Pete's a good guy," he says and I hear a noise from Kaidan at the table. Will and I both turn our attention to him.

"Did you say something?" I ask him. He shakes his head quickly and places a forkful of pancake into his mouth innocently. I shrug and dish out my eggs.

"Is, er, Amber coming over today?" Will asks me awkwardly. I swivel my head to look at him so quickly that I feel a twinge in my neck.

"Why?" I ask.

"I, um, I was just wondering." He ruffles his hair. "Never mind." He quickly leaves the room in a fluster and I tilt my head to one side. I hear Kaidan chuckle.

"What was that about?" I ask him. Kaidan laughs again.

"Isn't it obvious?" he says. "He's got a thing for your friend." I step back, repulsed.

"Ew!" I say. "My best friend and my brother? No, thank you."

"You asked, Gracie," he puts his hands up in the air as if to surrender. Then, like clockwork, the doorbell rings. I open it to see my two best friends standing at the door, beaming at me.

"Homecoming day!" they say enthusiastically, doing jazz moves with their hands. Oh god, what have I gotten myself into?

*   *   *

Amber has the day beginning with her fake tan. Why I need to fake tan is beyond me. But here I am, standing almost stark naked (almost, don't worry) covered in strange brown mousse.

"This smells weird," Jacob says, eyeing his brown arm. "And are you sure we leave it on for this long?"

I nod, agreeing with him.

"Yes, it smells like biscuits, and yes, we leave it on for another five minutes," Amber snaps. I idly wonder if she's going to be an event planner when she's older, with all her organizational skills. "Then we shower it off."

"Can't wait," I mumble, causing Amber to look over at me with eagle eyes. I raise my hands up, but she simply tells me to stay still or the tan will smudge.

Ten minutes is finally up and we take it in turns to shower off the brown mousse. I'll give it to her when it comes to beauty, Amber really knows what she's doing. The mousse has left me a golden-brown color, alluding to a recent holiday to the Bahamas. In reality, I haven't seen the sun since summer.

"I look fabulous!" Jacob announces, walking into my room in his boxers. I laugh as I watch him strut around the room like Beyoncé, his little behind wiggling as he walks.

"I told you!" Amber tells us then clapping her hands together. "Get dressed. It's time for hair." I glance at the clock to see that it's already past lunchtime and I'm suddenly glad Amber has us on such a tight schedule. Beauty takes time!

We arrive at Javi's hair salon with a minute to spare, according to Amber. Jacob embraces his boyfriend charismatically before gesturing to us to come in. The salon brings back memories of my first makeover. I smile, wondering what that Grace would think about everything that is happening now.

Thoughts of Uncle Jared have been at the back of my mind for most of the day. Everything with my family is back to normal, as if the whole dissociative amnesia thing never happened but it did, and I'm still lost in what actually happened the night that Jared was killed.

"Your turn, Grace," Jacob tells me, his hair in a perfect quiff. I snap out of my toxic thoughts and sit on the chair.

"What sort of look are you going for?" Javi asks me, eyeing up my hair. I ponder for a second before realizing that he knows a lot more than me.

"Just something elegant, I guess. Just work your magic," I tell him.

"Your wish is my command, beautiful," he tells me with a wink, before getting on with my hair. He works quickly and before I know it, he's holding a mirror behind me. My hair looks beautiful, curls in all the right places framing my face.

"Thank you," I tell him, before stepping out of the chair so Amber can have her hair done. She goes with a more elaborate look, curls everywhere and some gold flowers placed strategically to match her golden dress. She looks beautiful.

Hair done. We all climb back into Jacob's car and return to my house. My parents give us questioning looks as we rush through the kitchen, bags of makeup in hand.

"My favorite part!" Amber squeals, seeming a lot less flustered than she did earlier. We all take our stations by mirrors, before beginning the final step in our homecoming makeovers.

I immediately start on my face. I decide to not do anything too dramatic with my eyes but wear a red lipstick to match my dress. Amber, on the other hand, is watching a YouTube video and placing gold glitter on her eyelids. I wish I had her skills.

I put my red dress and shoes on, pulling the whole outfit all together. I wander over to the mirror to inspect myself, making sure the dress fits okay. To finish my look, I grab the beautiful pair of earrings Mom got me from Paris and put them on, the matching bracelet to follow.

"Finish!" I announce to my friends. Jacob buttons up his jacket and gives me a grin.

"You are so gorgeous, Grace," he says, giving me an air kiss on the cheek. Amber places her shoes on before glancing up at me. She looks like a Greek goddess.

"You look amazing!" we say in unison. And in this moment, I realize that the weight loss was not all about revenge. It was about becoming normal, and having this life with amazing friends.

"I love you guys," I tell them, wrapping my arms around both of them. They say it back. Then we realize Pete will be here any moment. Butterflies invade my stomach as we wander down the stairs.

My family plus Kaidan are still sitting at the table. Dad and Kaidan are immersed in deep conversation, probably about their project. All heads turn towards me and I see Kaidan's mouth drop.

The little devil on my shoulder smirks and cheers, telling me that he has the hots for me. The angel on the other side giggles and tells me it's probably just because I look different than usual.

I ignore them both. "What do you think?" I say, popping one leg in to pose.

138

"Oh Grace, you look beautiful," Mom gushes. "Jacob, Amber, you look marvelous!"

"I hate to say it, but yeah, you brush up good," Will teases, before getting up and wrapping an arm around my waist. He squeezes me tighter. I look up at him to see that his eyes are on Amber and his cheeks are red. I internally want to vomit.

Kaidan is glaring at me from across the table. Glaring or staring? I can't tell the difference between the two. Let's just hope it's the latter.

The silence is broken by the sound of the doorbell ringing. I become alert and rush to the door, opening it to find a suit-clad Pete. He's holding roses and his mouth drops when he sees me. I blush again and lean forward to give him a hug. I feel his lips on my cheek and I silently pray he doesn't see me blushing.

He holds out the rose. "Wow, Grace. You look beautiful." I grin and gladly take the flowers.

"They're beautiful. Thank you." I smile. "Come in. I'll just put these in a vase." My family remains in the kitchen—Mom ogling at Pete's face, Dad smiling in a proud way, Will eyeing Pete up, and Kaidan being stoic. But I can tell there's some emotion because I can see his fists clenching under the table. I feel a little victorious.

I place the roses in a vase on the table and as I lean over, I see Kaidan's eyes dart downwards. But he regains his cool and those unfeeling eyes connect with mine.

"Okay, we need to go!" Amber says, looking at the clock on the wall. "Homecoming time!"

139

TWENTY-SIX

I'll admit it, the Jistie has really outdone itself this time. The gymnasium has been transformed, covered in blue and silver décor. I clutch onto Pete's arm (mainly to stop myself from falling over in these ridiculous heels) as we wander through the crowd. Lucas is nowhere to be seen, fortunately. I've been avoiding him since the serenading incident and I have no plans in bumping into him tonight.

"Punch?" Pete offers me a glass filled with orange liquid.

"Thanks." I take a sip and silently wish that it contained alcohol. But alas, the drinking age is twenty-one and I am extremely far off.

"How's everything with you then?" Pete asks me as he takes a sip of his punch. He grimaces at the sweetness.

"I'm good." That is, apart from the amnesia. And Granddad. And Kaidan, whose mood fluctuates on the daily. I don't tell Pete those, though. Play the normalcy card. Fake it until you make it.

"Good," he nods. "I'm glad you agreed to come with me."

"Me too. Thanks for asking me." I smile at him and take another sip of punch. Oh, gross. Pete laughs at my reaction.

"Yeah, it's gross." He places his cup down on the table and I copy his action. That much sugar is not good for a previously obese girl, let's remember. I scan the room once more to see whether Lucas and his posse have arrived. Thankfully, they're nowhere to be seen.

"You seem on edge," Pete observes, raising an eyebrow. "Everything okay?"

"Yeah. I haven't seen Lucas since the whole confrontation thing. I'm anxious about seeing him, I guess," I tell him, rubbing my hands together anxiously.

"I see. I'm here to protect you, so you're good." He winks, making me laugh. "You have a beautiful smile, Grace."

My heart booms. "Thank you." *Boom. Boom. Boom.* It's so loud that I wonder whether Pete can hear it. I hope not.

"I've been meaning to ask you for a while, but—"

"Shit!" slips out of my mouth, interrupting Pete. It's unintentional, but I can't help it. Lucas just walked through the doors and his eyes are directly on me. Pete looks confused following my gaze.

"Oh, really?" Pete says as Lucas approaches us. He's wearing an extravagant tux, his bowtie bright blue.

"Looking lovely, Grace." Lucas cocks his head to one side. "Can't say the same about you, Alridge." He reaches his arm out and straightens Pete's bow tie. "You could have at least picked someone who knows how to dress himself."

I don't even know what to say. Does he not remember what I said to him in this very room a couple of days ago?

"Leave her alone, Lucas," Pete says through gritted teeth. The words only bring amusement to Lucas who turns to his posse.

"He thinks he's stronger than me. Everyone loves a tryer," he jokes to his friends who all laugh. "Apparently Gracie does." Anger ignites as he uses Kaidan's nickname for me.

"Don't call me that," I snap. Lucas' smile only grows bigger, sickening me.

"But it's so cute, don't you think?" Lucas turns his attention to Pete whose face is stormy. "Don't you agree with me,

Alridge?" he says Pete's last name patronizingly. Pete narrows his eyes.

"Go and bother someone else. Neither of us wants to speak to you." Pete flicks his hand at Lucas, but Lucas' smile doesn't falter.

"I'm sure Gracie has a couple of things to say to me, don't you?" He smirks at me before reaching out and pinching my cheek. I realize now that he's drunk.

"I think I was pretty clear last time." I try to match his composure, but on the inside, my nerves are coiling like snakes. "Or would you like me to reiterate?"

"Surely, you've got more than that? All those years bullying you and only a couple of sentences? Come on, Gracie, give it to me," he taunts, and I realize that he's trying to get a reaction out of me. Pete cups my elbow in an attempt to take me away from Lucas. "Hey hey hey! What's the rush?" Lucas jeers as he watches Pete's actions. Pete looks like he's about to explode with anger. I cut in before he says something he regrets.

"You know what I find funny, Lucas?" I ask and Lucas snaps his head back to me. "I find it funny how you thought that you ever had a chance with me."

"Oh really?" Lucas slurs. "And what's so funny about that?"

"It's funny, because according to evolutionary psychology, females are the choosy sex. That means we get to be the picky ones while you boys dance around trying to attract our attention. You could be like a bird and perform a dance to attract my attention. And I guess that's what you did, singing that ridiculous Justin Bieber song to me. But here's the catch—sexual selection is all about genetic quality. And Lucas, I'm afraid that behind that dyed blond hair, you really don't have that much to offer. You're dumb, unkind, rude, and you're not even that attractive. Lastly, everyone knows what a big personality is compensating for . . . and no one wants that in a mate. So, if your puny brain can understand the

142

words I just said, I think you'll realize it's time to leave me alone. Or I will continue to bore you with facts about how you're destined to end up alone," I finish, the tone in my voice identical to Lucas' taunts. He looks at me with cloudy eyes, the smile on his face earlier completely gone.

"You're just 'fat Grace'. No one even cares about you." That's the only comeback Lucas can muster. I smirk at him in a way that only he can mirror.

"And you're just that boy who was humiliated, not once, not twice, but three times by 'just fat Grace'." I use my fingers as quotation marks. "Goes to show what kind of guy you are." I don't wait for his reaction and simply turn around and walk away from him.

That, my friend, is what you call sweet revenge.

*   *   *

"You are fricking awesome, hunny," Jacob tells me as I approach him and Amber. I exhale heavily and roll my eyes.

"Don't even get me started." I place my hand on my forehead. "Did you see all of it?" I reflect on my words to Lucas Keith. Did I really use psychology to sass him out?

"Hell yeah! I recorded it." Amber wiggles her phone and I groan. How embarrassing. "Don't be embarrassed. It was so cool. He was at a loss for words," my best friend tells me.

"Just please tell me you decided to bring your hip flask," I murmur so my voice is hidden by the music. I know I'm not the type of person to break the school rules, let alone the law, but to get through this homecoming, I really need some of the devil's juice. Students always manage to get away with drinking at prom, so why should we be any different?

"I brought more than a hip flask," Amber winks at me. "Follow me." She takes my hand and leads me through a white door. Somehow, I lost Pete when I stormed away from Lucas so I make a note to go and find him after I've had a drink.

"Tada!" Amber says as we enter a kitchen, where three bottles of gin sit on the counter. I look at her in confusion.

"One of the guys in the gym fancies the pants off me," she says, flicking her gorgeous blonde hair behind her. "Turns out, he's on the catering team for tonight. He smuggled these in for me." I shake my head at her. She's marvelous.

"Dig in, my lovelies." She passes me a bottle of gin. I raise an eyebrow at her.

"No mixer?" I ask, watching her as she unscrews a bottle and flicks the lid off. She brings the bottle to her lips and takes a large gulp.

"I'm not weak, honey," she mimics Jacob who rolls his eyes at her. I hold my bottle up to Jacob's, clinking them before we each take a small sip. The liquid burns my throat as it slides down, before creating a warmth at the bottom of my stomach.

This is not going to end well.

∗   ∗   ∗

I am holding it together pretty well for someone who has had about ten shots of gin. Amber appears to still be sober (I need to learn to be able to hold my drink like she does) and Jacob is rolling around on the floor laughing.

"Ladies, we need to go back and join in!" I murmur to the two divas. Amber sticks her bottom lip out.

"But I'm not drunk!" she says but the last word slurs a little, indicating that she's more drunk than we both thought.

"Yes, you are. Let's go!" I demand, pulling Jacob from the floor and grabbing Amber's wrist. As we join the rest of the school, the songs are beginning to slow down and couples are beginning to form.

"May I have this dance?" Jacob puts both his hands out for us to take and just like twelve-year-old girls, we giggle and take a hand each. He swirls us around before pulling us in, having a three-way slow dance.

"May I steal Grace?" comes Pete's voice from my left. I give him a big grin before abandoning my friends and taking his hand.

"Bye then!" Amber calls while Jacob sniggers. I roll my eyes. Idiots.

"I have a suspicion," Pete says into my ear as we dance, swaying in unison.

"And what's that?" I giggle, before spinning myself out of his arms and twirling back in. He laughs at my drunk behavior.

"I think that you may be drunk," he chuckles. I twirl one more time, heavily thudding into his chest. Couples around us give me looks but I don't care. They're just jealous.

"What gave you that impression?" I ask him, swaying in his arms. He pulls me closer and tucks a strand of hair behind my ear.

"I think it's pretty obvious," he whispers, making chills run down my spine. The familiar feeling of butterflies in my stomach swirl as we dance.

"I have another suspicion," he says, moving his face from over my shoulder so that we make eye contact. I tilt my head to one side, curious.

He takes a deep breath. "I suspect that I might be falling in love with you, Grace Connely."

TWENTY-SEVEN

"You what?" comes out of my mouth. Pete puts his finger to my lips and shushes me.

"I don't want you to say anything. It's been on my mind and I wanted to get it off my chest." He gives me a half smile. "I would love to kiss you though if that's allowed." I almost step backwards in shock. I've never kissed anyone before. Is Pete going to be that person? I can almost hear Amber in my thoughts, yelling at me to kiss him. 'He likes you, you idiot,' she'd be saying.

"Okay," I manage to say, closing my eyes. I feel like I'm waiting forever until his lips finally touch mine. He's soft at first, as if he worries he'll scare me off. Once I return his kiss, he becomes more passionate, deepening the kiss. I follow his lead, unsure of what I'm doing. But the way our lips mold together, I have a feeling I'm doing something right. When we pull away, he traces a finger down my cheek and gives me a big smile.

"You really are one of a kind." He smiles and we continue to dance as my heart thumps in my chest. When the song stops, Principal Keith climbs up onto the stage at the front.

"It's that time of the night, folks!" he announces over the microphone. Ugh, I groan internally. I don't even think the numbing effects of alcohol will make homecoming king and queen any easier. It's probably just going to be Lucas and some blonde cheerleader.

"First of all, I'm going to read out our homecoming king nominees," the principal announces, pulling out a piece of paper. "Lucas Keith." Surprise surprise. "Andy Warkins and Jacob Sanders." What the . . . I look over at Jacob whose mouth is wide open. To his right, Amber is almost wetting herself with laughter. He reluctantly and drunkenly follows the other nominees onto the stage.

"And now for our homecoming queen nominees," Principal Keith clears his throat, "Sadie Admans." Classic captain of the cheerleaders. "Penelope Cartwright. Grace Connely!"

It's my turn to drop my mouth open. I spin around to see Amber, who is, once again, in hysterics. I shake my head at her before begrudgingly following the rest of the nominees up. Jacob is now seeing the funny side of it and is laughing his head off on stage. I narrow my eyes at Lucas whose facial expression is difficult to read.

"Our homecoming king and queen are . . ." Principal Keith unfolds the slip containing this year's big winners.

"Lucas Keith and Grace Connely!" he announces and my stomach drops. Is this a joke? But everyone is applauding and so I hesitantly walk to the center of the stage where Mrs. Fatimiah places the tiara on my head.

"Well done, sweetie," she tells me. Shock waves ripple through me, then I feel a hand taking mine. I almost recoil when I see that it is Lucas, but I don't want to ruin the tradition so we hold our hands up and bow.

"I'm going to make your life a living hell, Grace Connely," Lucas whispers in my ear. I wish I had known what he meant.

*   *   *

"Well, hello miss homecoming queen!" Amber cheers as I finally leave the stage bearing my crown and sash. I feel ridiculous.

"It's your fault for nominating me!" I say, and she puts her hands up in surrender.

"I only nominated Jacob, hun. Lucas must have done it. He was expecting to come to homecoming with you after all," Amber says. My blood boils as Lucas' parting words run through my mind. *I'm going to make your life a living hell.*

"Well, that all came back to hit him in the ass, didn't it?" I roll my eyes, trying to get any thoughts of my bully off my brain. "I need some more gin. That seriously sobered me up."

"Can I get in on that?" Pete wraps his arms around my waist and gives me a kiss on the cheek. "Well done on getting homecoming queen." I smack him playfully.

"Let's never talk of this again," I say to all of them, receiving looks of approval from Amber, whose eyes are firmly on Pete's arms which are around my waist.

"Gin it is then!" Jacob cheers, and we all rush into the kitchen and grab the bottles of gin. Amber claps her hands together theatrically.

"Let's play a drinking game!" she cheers. "No scrooges, please. We are playing never have I ever," she says and I don't argue. It could be fun.

"Never have I ever kissed anyone in this room," she begins, directing her question at me. I sigh and take a swig of gin, pass the bottle to Pete, who then takes his swig after me. Both Amber and Jacob cheer, making me and Pete laugh.

"My turn," I say, thinking for a moment. "Never have I ever dated Lucas Keith," I direct the question back at Amber who pouts and takes a big sip of her drink.

"Not fair. I was naïve and stupid." She shrugs. "Jacob, your turn." Jacob is evidently still very drunk from our last drinking period and is rolling on the floor again.

"Sometimes, when I close my eyes, I pretend to be a chicken nugget." Jacob coos as he wriggles around the floor.

There's a moment of silence before we all burst out in hysterics at Jacob's strange behavior.

"Never have I ever," Jacob shouts over our laughter, "been a homecoming queen!" I sigh once again as the question is directed at me. Are they trying to get me drunk?

"You'll always be my queen, baby." I wink at him before taking a long sip of gin. Okay now I'm drunk. Pete clears his throat and scratches his chin, pretending to be thinking.

"Never have I ever been nominated for homecoming king." Pete nudges my shoulder and I give him a drunken high five. Jacob just chuckles to himself.

"I'm a chicken nugget, not homecoming king." He wiggles once more. Amber stands up and wanders over to the so-called chicken nugget and moves him into a sitting position.

"I think that signifies that we need to go home." Amber wraps her arm around Jacob's waist. "I'll take him. You guys make your own way home. Just wish me luck." She looks at Jacob who is pretending to dip himself into ketchup. I laugh again at my ridiculous best friend before wishing Amber a drunken good luck and bidding my farewell.

"We should probably head home too. You're looking a little worse for wear," Pete jokes. I feel the room move slightly. I guess I'm drunker than I thought.

"Sounds *gooooood*." I giggle before boldly leaning forward and placing my lips onto Pete's. At first, he seems surprised but then he melts into the kiss. Then my feet fall from underneath me. Pete is quick to catch me.

"Time to go home," Pete says and I nod silently.

*　　*　　*

When Pete drops me off, he gives me an amazing kiss before returning to the cab and zooming out of my driveway. I feel like I'm in a movie. That is, until I hear the front door open and see Kaidan standing there in his boxers.

What the hell? I frown at him and giggle. The last round of gin only just hitting me.

"You're back very late, Gracie," he says, his voice sleepy and deep.

"So? What are you, my father?" I say and laugh way too much, considering that what I just said wasn't particularly funny. My laughter increases and I step into the house past Kaidan who looks incredibly confused.

"Are you drunk?" he says slowly.

"No, Mr. Policeman. I swear. Look I can walk in a straight line," I say, before attempting—and failing—to walk a couple of steps forward. My ankle goes over and Kaidan's sturdy arm is around me instantly.

"You are drunk. God Gracie." He puts me back on my feet and I laugh again.

"And you, Kaidan, are not really wearing very many clothes," I say, poking his stomach. When I realize it's like a rock, I run my hands all over it. Wow, it's so smooth! Kaidan groans and moves my hands back to my sides.

"I was in bed before you and that wannabe came back making a huge racket," he says sighing. "I wasn't asleep, anyway. I was too worried that he was going to kidnap you or something."

"Oh Kai. Don't be so silly," I say in a childish voice, pinching his cheeks. "Besides . . . why would the boy who's in love with me kidnap me?" I giggle. Kaidan's eyes suddenly dart up to meet mine.

"What?" he snaps. A little parade of cheerleaders in my head gives a cheer.

"Is it really that difficult to imagine someone being interested in me?" I pout. He shakes his head and runs his hand through his hair.

150

"Yes, actually. You're so bloody annoying," he says. I frown but the alcohol causes my mood to shift pretty quickly.

"So bloody annoying," I say in my best Australian accent. As it's appalling, I burst into a fit of laughter. "Oh, I make myself laugh."

"As I said, annoying."

I burst into another fit of giggles. Kaidan's cool eyes soften for a second and I reach up to touch his face. His stubble feels strange against my skin and I laugh again. I look up and see him close his eyes.

"Are you sleepy?" I whisper. Instead of answering me, he just takes my hand in his and removes it from his face. For a second, we just stand there with him holding my hand lightly. I reach up and I place my lips on his cheek.

"I'm not afraid of the big bad wolf," I whisper in his ear. "You're a big softy really." And with that, I try to elegantly make my way up the stairs. Failing, I trip over. Obviously Kaidan catches me and I feel his breathing close to my cheek.

"Oh, but little Red, what a big heart you have." He presses his lips to my cheek. "Don't let Pete find out where it actually lies." He places me on my feet and swaggers upstairs, leaving my heart pounding.

Somehow, I manage to get myself into bed. I only manage to strip into my underwear though, leaving my beautiful dress on the floor. I collapse into bed, my head spinning.

Why is my heart suddenly torn? Tonight, I think about how I had feelings for Pete and that I hated Kaidan. He's mean and rude to me and he treats me like I'm so much younger than him. For Christ's sake, he's only a year older than me! Thoughts bubble around my head. Why did Kaidan have to say that? Is he still under the strange illusion that I'll fall in love with him? The way he acts around me . . . it's like he can't decide whether he likes me or not. I decide to blame all my weird thoughts on the alcohol and allow myself to drift to sleep.

TWENTY-EIGHT

Sunday. This means that tomorrow is Monday (my birthday yay!) and I'm lucky enough to have my birthday landing on a federal holiday, meaning no school. Whoopee!

The first thing I notice is my pounding headache. Oh, a hangover, how fantastic. I groan and roll around in my blue duvet, making use of the space from the double bed. I suddenly hear the door open and Kaidan wanders in with a glass of water.

"Morning. Thought you could do with a glass of water." He places it on the counter next to me. I sit up and realize I'm only in my ugly white underwear. Kaidan thankfully hasn't noticed (or so I think) so I just pull the duvet up to cover me completely. I glug down the water in a couple of sips, the result being water dribbling out the side of my mouth. Go Grace, you know exactly how to be attractive!

Kaidan chuckles and I feel that this is the first time in ages I've heard that sound. I laugh with him, appreciating the moment. That's when Kaidan suddenly chucks a pillow at me. I frown in utter confusion until I see him standing by the bed, his eyes crinkling at the corners. He's smiling for once. I don't say a sarcastic comment or anything, I simply laugh with him and chuck the pillow back. That's when he decides to grab the whole duvet and pull it off me. I keep laughing until I realize that he stops moving.

Sweet Jesus.

I'm lying in my underwear with Kaidan standing over me, staring at me. I mean, he's not even trying to hide it. I blush and cover my face with my hands. I impulsively reach for the bottom of the duvet but his arm stops me. My eyes widen as he sits on the edge of the bed. I wriggle around slightly, feeling very uncomfortable under his glare. What on earth is he doing?

"Do you remember last night?" he asks. "When you came back?"

"Vaguely," I mumble. That's a lie. I remember it very well. I remember stroking (yes stroking) his abs. I'm such an embarrassment to human society. I suddenly feel his hands on my stomach. They're warm and he moves them up slightly, but not too far up. I am completely paralyzed. I have no idea what to do. What is he doing? My mouth moves up and down, but no words come out, I bet I look like a fish.

He smirks as he takes them off. "Now we're even." With that, he leaves the room. I am left in utter confusion. That boy does weird things to my head. He acts really cold to me and then he acts like that . . .

I check my phone to see three messages. Two are from Amber, both of which contain videos of Jacob dancing around her kitchen at 3 a.m. pretending to be a chicken nugget. I laugh at the memory and save them to my phone. The other is from Pete.

I had an awesome time last night. I'll see you at school x

I smile at the sweet message and respond quickly before climbing out of bed. I pull on an oversized tee before making my way downstairs. Kaidan and Will are having breakfast and I eye it hungrily. Kaidan is staring at me. Well, more specifically, my legs. Dammit, I should have put leggings on.

"Morning Grace," Will chirps and I give him a smile as I wander over to the fridge. My hangover hunger causing my stomach to make some bizarre noises.

154

"Morning. Is there any bacon left? It's my hangover remedy," I ask him and he nods.

"Yeah, Kaidan put it in the oven for you when he came downstairs," he tells me. I look over at Kaidan whose gaze is still on my legs. I pretend I don't notice, going over to the oven and putting the oven mitts on.

Oh no. I'm either going to have to bend over or crouch down to take the bacon out. Both of which will expose my underwear. Wow, nice going Grace!

I glance behind me and this time, Kaidan's eyes are on mine. He smirks but doesn't tear his eyes from me. Feeling bold, I crouch down and open the oven. As expected, the tee rises and I feel my underwear go on display. I take the bacon out and return to standing. I look over at Kaidan who is staring right at me with fists clenched under the table.

The small band of cheerleaders do a little routine in my head and its now my turn to smirk. Ah hell, I even throw in a small wink at his direction. I see him narrow his eyes as if to say, 'two can play that game'. He wets his lips with his tongue and even from our distance, I see his eyes drop down to my lips.

My eyes widen in surprise, but I quickly regain my cool and push a blonde strand of hair behind my ear. I allow my eyes to drift down to his lips before turning away and reaching up to the cupboard with the plates inside. While all that has been going on, Will has been completely oblivious. I make a bacon sandwich before sitting down at the table opposite Kaidan. Thankfully, Will leaves the room, muttering something about doing some work.

Kaidan is still staring at me. "What are you doing, Gracie?" he growls. What is he, a tiger?

"I don't know what you're talking about," I say, feigning innocence. His eyes darken and he places his mug down.

"Yes, you do," he murmurs, leaning forward so his face is close to mine.

"I told you, I'm not afraid of the Big Bad Wolf," I reply, bringing my face close to his. My heart is beating at a ridiculous rate and I'm scared it's going to burst out of my chest. What am I doing? Just last night I was kissing Pete.

"Oh no, you're not afraid of me. But you're afraid of your feelings for me, aren't you Gracie?" he says in a hoarse voice. I smirk.

"Just as you are for me." I bring my face even closer to his. "I see the way you look at me, Kai. I see your jealousy of Pete. Admit it. You have feelings for me."

"You're wrong," he mutters. My heart drops but I don't believe him. I've never been looked at the way he looks at me.

"Oh, am I?" I murmur, before slowly pressing my lips on his cheek, dangerously close to his lips. I hear his breath catch in his throat and I smile, pulling away.

"Just as I thought." I saunter away from him with my bacon sandwich, swaying my hips as I go.

*   *   *

I decide to ring Amber and see if she and Jacob want to come over for my birthday. They are my best friends after all.

Ring ring. Ring ring. "Grace!" I hear her squeal on the other end of the phone. I smile. Even after a night of heavy drinking, she still sounds chirpy.

"Hey Ambs, how you doing?" I ask, before taking a bite of the yumminess of my sandwich.

"I'm outrageously hungover, but I think the real topic here is that it's your eighteenth tomorrow! Woohoo!" she cheers. I grin and laugh at her enthusiasm. She never fails to cheer me up.

"I was wondering if you and Jacob could come over for the celebration. I'd really love it if you could," I ask her and I hear a squeal.

156

"Of course! I'll bring loads of stuff," she cheers again. "Okay, I'll tell Jacob right this second. Love you Grace, bye!"

"Love you too," I tell her before I hang up. I hear Kaidan coming up the stairs. I turn around and sit on the bed so I'm facing him when he reaches my room.

As expected, he comes into my room but he's seething with anger. My eyes widen in surprise.

"What the hell was that about Gracie?" he fumes. "You can't just do that then walk away." He slams the door shut behind him. I'm startled, I wasn't expecting him to react like this.

"So, you're admitting that you have feelings for me?" I tease, trying to keep the mood as lighthearted as I can but miserably failing.

"You don't get to choose if I have feelings for you, Gracie. I make that call," he says, anger evident in his voice. I tilt my head to one side and stand up. He walks over to me, so our bodies are nearly touching and my heart rate accelerates.

"And have you made that call yet? Because I'm sick of you acting one way then a moment later acting completely differently." My mood switches from teasing to anger. Kaidan runs his hands through his hair and takes a step towards me, swearing under his breath.

"The only reason I act that way is because I'm trying to stop myself from kissing you."

TWENTY-NINE

I'm in shock and our bodies are now touching. I take deep breaths to stop myself from hyperventilating. My eyes have increased to the size of saucepans in my state of shock. He just keeps on surprising me. The boy that has been aggravating me for the past couple of months, who I thought hated me . . . wants to kiss me.

A whirlwind of thoughts erupts in my mind and I look up to meet Kaidan's eyes. Something raw flashes through them, before glancing down to my lips.

"You, uh, want to kiss me?" I ask, trying to regain my calm. A smirk grows on his face and he nods slowly.

"For a while now," he says softly, his eyes growing dark. I swallow awkwardly and breathe out.

"Oh yeah. Cool. Great. Um," I stammer awkwardly, having completely lost my cool demeanor. His smirk grows bigger and he lowers his head, so our lips are nearly touching.

Our eyes are still connected, but for some reason mine flutter shut, and that's when I feel it. His soft lips press against mine and I let out a sigh of relief.

It's as if all the air has been sucked out of the room and I'm his oxygen. He's suddenly kissing me deeply and it's better than I ever imagined.

He kisses me hungrily before pushing me backwards so I land on the bed. Climbing on top of me, he brings his head back down to kiss me again. I run my hands through his hair, then tug, trying to get him closer to me. He moves his hand up my bare thigh and across my stomach. A small sound escapes from my lips and I feel Kaidan smile in response. His hand travels up to my face, caressing my cheeks and tugging slightly at my hair. He suddenly pulls away and I immediately think that he's regretted kissing me.

He's staring at me in a way I just can't comprehend, so I sit up. We stare at each other for a while before he puts his hands on either side of my waist and pulls me onto his lap. I smile down at him and bring my lips to his neck. In all honesty, I have absolutely no idea what I'm doing, but from the way he's responding to me, I can tell it's good.

When I pull away, he's already panting heavily and my heart rate is booming. We stare at each other, hair disheveled. He scratches his chin before breaking our eye contact. His eyes dart around the floor and my heart rate accelerates. What is he thinking? God, I wish I knew what he's thinking. He frowns and still doesn't meet my eyes.

"Dammit," he says and runs his hands through his hair, "I know that you, uh, have feelings for me. But in answer to your question, no, I do not share them. You're very attractive, but that's it." He then stands up and leaves the room. When the door shuts, despair pools through me.

What?

I should have known that would happen. How could I be so stupid?

*   *   *

I stay hidden in my room all day. Embarrassment has consumed me. Why on earth would Kaidan be interested in me? Why would I even thought that for a second? He is basically a Greek god and I am . . . an ex-fat girl who has serious insecurity issues.

I send a text to Amber and Jacob telling them to come over as soon as possible. I need to talk to both of them. I need to tell them what's going on with Kaidan. And Pete. God, what have I gotten myself into?

The kiss comes back to my mind. The feeling of his lips on mine is still there and anger boils within me. I don't think I'm the one with the psychological disorder. It's most definitely him. His mood is all over the place. One day he's being friendly, laughing with me, the next he's . . . Kaidan. I was stupid to think that he may have changed for me.

I hate him. He has managed to make me feel worthless in the space of about ten minutes. I lean back down onto the bed and bury my face in a pillow. I hate boys.

All of a sudden, I feel a tear trickle down my cheek. Am I . . . crying? I wipe it away quickly, but more tears gather in my eyes to replace the ones I tried to get rid of. Sobs begin to rack through me and I feel an uncontrollable sadness take over me.

How dare he say he doesn't share my feelings for him.

How dare he kiss me.

How dare he make me feel wanted and then throw it in my face.

I hate the fact that I enjoyed the kiss.

I hate the fact he is living in my house.

But what I hate most is the fact that I don't hate him. I don't hate him at all. And that is what hurts me the most.

I stand up and glance at myself in the mirror. I am not weak. Those boys do not control me. But seeing myself in the mirror—this fragile human being with dark rings under her eyes—I realize they have completely taken over my life.

And in this moment, I decide that I want Kaidan to feel the pain I'm feeling. I shouldn't be acting like some damaged girl. He did this to me. Now I just need to return the favor.

THIRTY

After showering and cleaning myself up, I no longer look like a mess. I practice my you-have-not-just-made-me-feel-like-a-piece-of-dirt smile in the kitchen. I try to imitate Kaidan's smirk. Nothing like a bit of arrogance to set the mood.

I put on some black ripped jeans and a white shirt before sauntering downstairs. Keep your cool, Grace. You've got this.

Kaidan is having lunch by himself. Perfect. I deflect away the pang of feelings that hit me when I see him. The cheerleaders in my head have placed their pom poms down and are sitting in despair. I internally frown at them. Pick yourself together girls!

He looks up and gives me a strange look. As if he expects me to be sad or something. I may be embarrassed, but I know better than to let him control my emotions. I give him the smirk I practiced in the mirror and he furrows his eyebrows in response.

"You okay?" he asks but the tone is dead, much like it was when I first met him. Like I'm an afterthought. Anger runs through my veins and I narrow my eyes.

"Yeah, I'm good." I smile innocently. "You?"

My reaction has completely baffled him, I can tell. He has completely stopped eating. "Yeah fine. Are you having lunch?"

"Of course. I'll wait until you're gone of course." I fold my arms, watching as confusion etches across that beautiful face. *Bad Grace*. I tell myself. He's not beautiful. He's an ass.

161

"Er, why?" he asks with his eyes locked on mine. I don't break the contact and bring the smirk back to my lips again.

"Because the idea of eating in the same room as you makes me feel slightly nauseous," I say, grimacing slightly. "That kiss," I mock a gag, "let's not do that again, okay?"

The look on his face is priceless and my smirk grows bigger. I see a slight flush on his face before he chuckles. "Gracie, you definitely enjoyed that kiss."

Yes, you're right.

"Sure, I did. And I also enjoy your company," I say sarcastically. He rolls his eyes and saunters around the counter so that he's closer to me.

"You're mad about what I said, aren't you? That's why you're acting like this," he concludes and looks pleased with himself.

I laugh. "You couldn't be more wrong. I'm actually really glad we're on the same page now. Don't want you falling in love with me now, do I?" I use his line. Ha. I laugh in the face of danger. His face grows stony and he abruptly stands up. He marches over to me and places his hands on either side of the work surface next to me.

"I would never." He brings his face down to mine. *Oh, I wish I could kiss him.* I slap myself internally. I need to get myself out of this infatuation with Kaidan.

"I would appreciate it if you got out of my face, Kaidan," I say coolly. He narrows his eyes and pushes himself away from me.

"Okay Gracie, have it your way," he says, confusion still evident on his face. I shoo him away and push myself off the counter too. As he wanders away, I admire his behind.

Kaidan, why do you do this to me?

*　　*　　*

I text Amber and Jacob, asking them to come over. I need to see them sooner to figure out this mess with Pete and Kaidan. A week ago, I hadn't even touched a boy (apart from Jacob, of course). Now I've kissed two, in the space of two days. *What a hoe.* My internal voice murmurs at me, and I want to slap it. It's a free country!

The doorbell rings and I dart downstairs to answer it. Seeing Amber and Jacob's beaming faces, I launch myself into both their arms in happiness. I need a little more positivity in my life. I drag them both to my room immediately and collapse onto the bed.

"Why do I feel like we're about to have a threesome?" Jacob inquires, and I hit him. That boy can be perverted sometimes.

"So, Grace," Amber says, "what's going on?"

"So, Pete told me he's falling in love with me at homecoming," I say, and they both gasp. I chuckle in response. They're both so dramatic.

"You're joking," Jacob says with a shocked expression. I shake my head and feel a slight blush rise to my cheeks.

"Do you like him?" Amber asks, her tone very serious. I just shrug.

"I thought I did. But then . . . I don't know, I'm feeling very conflicted." I pause and take a deep breath. Here goes nothing. "Kaidan kissed me."

Silence fills the room. I avoid both their intense stares. "Is she joking? She must be joking, right?" Jacob whispers to Amber. I look up, and Amber is staring at me.

"Guys, please don't judge," I mumble awkwardly.

"No babe. We're not judging," Jacob says nicely. I give him a small smile and look back at Amber's face which has confusion all over it.

"Grace, I'm not judging you," she says quietly. Wow, I never thought I'd use that word to describe Amber. "It's more that I'm worried you don't look the slightest bit happy about it."

Her words break me. All the feelings I pushed away in the last hour come rushing back and my eyes begin to gather tears again. My best friends' eyes widen and sit next to me.

"What happened?" Jacob coos, wrapping his arm around my shoulder.

"After we kissed, he told me he doesn't 'share' my feelings for him," I mumble, a tear silently trickling down my cheek. God, I am so weak.

"Oh Grace," Amber says, taking my hand, "you don't deserve that."

"I hate feeling this weak," I tell them, wiping tears away from my cheeks. "So earlier I decided to pretend I hated the whole thing and that I hate him." I bite my lip. "But I just don't."

"Right." Jacob clasps his hands together. "I'm going downstairs to get popcorn. Amber, put Mean Girls on. Grace, put your pj's on."

And so, I do. We eat and eat and eat. Watch movie after movie. Having my friends comforting me is the best thing in the world and Kaidan is almost off my mind.

THIRTY-ONE

Amber and Jacob stay the night but when I wake up, they're gone. I frown and sit up. They suddenly both burst in, Amber holding a cake and Jacob holding a happy birthday banner. I grin—I almost forgot it was my birthday.

And Kaidan's . . .

I push the unwanted thought away and blow out the candles. I wish for a fresh start. My two best friends are clapping ecstatically and I grin at them. In my room, we have cake for breakfast. Screw my diet. I can eat badly for a couple of days.

Amber and Jacob have given me a joint present and they both look incredibly excited to give it to me. In my eager anticipation, I hastily unwrap it and see a beautiful silver frame with a picture of us three. We're laughing at something and I have no idea when it was taken but it warms my heart. At the bottom of the frame, they have engraved in a swirly font:

We'll be there for you, through thick and thin x

Tears form in my eyes and I wrap an arm around both of them. "Thank you so much guys. I love it." I put it up on my side table so it's always close to me.

The two of them decide to go home and leave me with my family for the rest of the day. I just hope I can avoid Kaidan at all

165

costs. After they've gone, I take a shower and make myself look presentable. It is my birthday after all.

I wander downstairs to see Will and my parents having breakfast. They all beam at me and get up to give me happy birthday hugs straightaway.

After another round of *happy birthday to you*, I make myself a coffee and sit down with them. I am so glad Kaidan isn't awake. I don't want to face him quite yet.

My parents pass a present to me, their smiles taking up most of their faces. I can tell they're excited about giving it to me. It's a small box, so I hastily open it, expecting it to be some form of jewelry. As I open the box, I shriek.

It's a car key! I bounce over to both of them in excitement and give them a kiss on the cheek before dashing outside to see a silver Golf with a huge bow on it. I hear my parents laughing in the background as they watch me sprint over to it and climb in.

It smells amazing and I start the engine immediately. I drive it around our driveway for a couple of minutes just to have a feel.

Climbing back out, I run over and give them each another huge hug, showering them with thank yous. From their beaming smiles, I can tell that they're happy that I'm happy.

When I stumble back into the kitchen, Kaidan is standing by the table. My heartbeat quickens and I nervously bite my lip before regaining my cool demeanor. I give him that smirk I was practicing before settling down at the table.

"Happy birthday Gracie," he says coldly. Hmph. Grumpy Kaidan is on the menu today. I don't look at him because I'm worried that if I do, I'll cry. I don't return the message. He doesn't deserve my attention.

"Happy birthday bro," Will says as he gives Kaidan a manly hug. I briefly look up to see Kaidan smiling with Will. God, why can't he just be like that around me? He suddenly sees me looking and immediately his smile falters.

I take a deep breath. Don't cry, Grace. Stay strong. I look down, away from Kaidan's harsh glare. I swallow, attempting to stop tears from falling but one quickly escapes and drips down my cheek. I internally curse and hastily wipe it away.

I keep my gaze directed at the table. I know Kaidan is still glaring at me. When my tears have disappeared, I look back up to see my dad handing Kaidan a check, muttering an awkward happy birthday, telling him to not spend it all at once and that it's a bonus for doing a really good job. Kaidan thanks him and his eyes find mine again.

Despite my sadness, I mask it by narrowing my eyes in a way Kaidan does to me all the time. *Happy birthday.*

I stand and dismiss myself. I sprint up to my room before tears begin to cascade down my cheeks. I hate this power he has over me. He's making me feel awful and I still have these intense feelings for him that I just wish would disappear.

I don't even realize the door has opened before I hear "Gracie" in that all too familiar Australian accent. I rub my face quickly in a vain attempt to not let him see my tears.

"Why are you crying?" he asks, the coldness still in his voice but his face is softer. I meet his eyes and shake my head.

"Er, I'm not," I stutter hopelessly. A small tear trickles down my cheek. Dammit. Kaidan's face suddenly falls and his eyebrows furrow.

"Yes, you are," he mumbles, before sitting on the bed next to me. I search my mind for an explanation to give him.

"I'm just happy with my car, that's all," I mumble, trying to smile a little. I know my lie entirely fails when I see his face. He doesn't believe me in the slightest.

"Those aren't happy tears," he says, "and I have a feeling they're my doing." His voice is very quiet for the last bit and something inside me cracks. Here come the waterworks.

167

"Don't flatter yourself. I'm fine Kaidan." I look down as a stream of tears falls down my cheeks. "Just go." For the love of God, these damn tears! Why am I so emotional?

"Why are you so mad at me?" Kaidan asks softly. I don't sense any coldness in his voice and I look up at him with red brimmed eyes.

"I'm not. Please leave." I muster the most courage I can but my voice is croaky and evidently sad. His eyes lose their coolness and he looks hopeless. He has no idea what to do—he almost looks . . . vulnerable.

"Gracie, please tell me," he asks. My head snaps up in anger.

"Why are you so goddam bipolar?" I seethe, adrenaline coursing through me. "One minute you act like you hate me with every last breath in your body, and then another you pretend like you actually care! Just pick one!" I'm fuming now and his eyes are wide.

"I'm not bipolar," he mutters quietly. And I laugh. I actually laugh. For someone who is supposed to be clever, he's acting really stupid.

"I wish I could explain it to you," he says, his eyes connecting with mine. "I just . . . I don't know how to act around you."

Well, I wasn't expecting that. He doesn't know how to act around me? What does that even mean? I'm left speechless but Kaidan carries on.

"You're my boss's daughter," he says lowly. "It's complicated."

I regain my voice and I'm even angrier now. "But you're nice to Will. Why can't you just treat me the same as Will?"

I hear him sigh. "Will is my friend. That's why I'm nice to him." Oh, ouch. So, we're not even friends now.

"Wow. Okay. I thought we could at least count this relationship as friendship, but evidently I was wrong." I seethe.

"No, Gracie. You're not getting it. We can't have the same relationship as I do with Will." He looks lost for words, a look I've never seen on him before.

"It would make everything so much easier if we could."

"I know it would." He pauses and his eyes meet mine. "But I don't have any sort of friendship feelings towards you, Gracie. That's where the problem lies."

Ouch, another slap in the face. "Thanks," I mutter, attempting to contain my anger. "Let's just agree to stay out of each other's way then," I say, forcing the words out.

"You're not getting it," he says irritably. All of a sudden, he's up and out of the room.

Okay then. My befuddlement is evaporated when he returns to the room with a rectangular present. He places it on my lap carefully. "Maybe this will make it clearer." Then he leaves.

He got me a birthday present? I unwrap it carefully to see an old covered book. It reads *Little Red Riding Hood* and under that it says *And The Big Bad Wolf.*

Confused, I open the large book. The author is 'Anonymous' and in the foreword, I see that the book is from the wolf's point of view.

Intrigued, I begin to read the familiar story turned on its head. The book is huge—it'll take me days to read it. But I'm determined to understand what Kaidan was trying to explain.

*   *   *

The rest of my birthday wizzes by in a blur. I receive numerous texts wishing me a happy birthday, including a soppy one from Lucas. I don't see Kaidan for the rest of the day and guilt is eating away at me about the fact that I didn't buy him a present.

My family and I eat my favorite meal while Kaidan's seat is empty and overbearing to me just by looking at it. I remain quiet. I'm so lost in my thoughts that I'm barely speaking to my family.

169

After finishing, I excuse myself and get to bed. I search frantically in my room trying to find something to give to Kaidan as a late birthday present. When I'm looking through my jewelry box, a silver signet ring catches my eye.

It was the one Amber was going to give Kyle for his birthday months ago, before realizing he hated jewelry. It's a signet ring and it has a K engraved on it. My excitement spikes and I hastily grab it and rush to Kaidan's room.

After knocking, he opens it wearily. His cold eyes are gone, and they're now . . . tender.

"I felt bad that I didn't get you a present," I mumble. "I found this, I thought it would be fitting." I pass him the ring and he takes it suspiciously. He gives me a small smile.

"Thanks, Gracie," he says. "I really like it." And suddenly I'm in his arms. He's hugging me tightly and it takes me a while to wrap my arms around him in reciprocation. We stand in silence, holding each other despite all the anger and hidden words between us.

And in that moment, I fall hopelessly, incandescently and irrevocably in love with Kaidan Micah.

THIRTY-TWO

My alarm bleeps through my dreams of Kaidan. Yes, I am completely in love with him and I cannot deny it anymore. I sigh and cover my face with my pillow in despair. He'll never get out of this infinitely bad mood with me.

I take a huge amount of care over my appearance. First, I'm going back to school today and second (the most important), Kaidan will be downstairs having breakfast already, so I want to look good.

God. What have I turned into?

I have a shower and blow dry my hair straight. No frizzy hair today for me. I apply a little makeup, not too dramatic, before pulling on some grey cigarette trousers, a white shirt and some heeled boots. I look smart and kind of chic at the same time. Nodding at my appearance in the mirror, I take a deep breath and wander downstairs.

As predicted, Kaidan is drinking coffee at the table, preparing to go to the office. I swoon. Look at his bone structure. I mean, he is a seriously beautiful specimen. He turns to look at me with furrowed eyebrows. I give him an awkward smile before scuttling over to the cupboard, my cheeks burning.

Why has my realization of my feelings for him made me act so differently around him? I wait for my cheeks to cool before taking two pop tarts out of the cupboard.

"Gracie, why are you the color of a tomato?" he asks, amusement evident in his voice. Dammit! I try to act normally.

"I'm not," I squeak, before rushing over to the toaster. Wow, smooth Grace. Real smooth.

"Okay then," he says slowly, and I don't have to turn around to know he's smirking. Oh, and what an attractive smirk that is . . .

Snap out of it, Grace! I scold myself, but my band of internal cheerleaders are all swooning too. I internally roll my eyes and groan.

Oh wait, I outwardly groaned. My pop tarts are done and I settle down opposite Kaidan. I feel his intense gaze and I look up to meet his eyes.

"Everything ok?" I say, my voice a little higher than usual. I cough, in order to give the impression there's something wrong with my voice.

"Well, considering I'm not the one acting like a lunatic, I would say yes," he chuckles, and I sit still. I haven't heard him laugh in ages. I blush, not because of what I said but because of the sound of his laugh. Grace, for frick sake, really?

"Why are you blushing so much?" he questions, before taking a sip of coffee. Good question, Kaidan! Because I am totally obsessed and in love with you! I internally hit myself again. I need to grow a pair of balls.

"I'm too hot," I manage through bites of pop tart. Okay, good answer. Perfectly understandable explanation to why I'm the color of a beetroot.

Kaidan mumbles something under his breath that is incoherent, so I just munch through my pop tart slowly, every so often bringing my gaze up to his beautiful face.

I could watch him all day. He's that gorgeous. Sure, call me a stalker, but my band of cheerleaders and I are really enjoying the show. They are currently undressing him with their eyes. I'm a lost cause.

When I've finished my pop tart, I look up to steal another glance at Kaidan but to my surprise, he's already staring at me. Have I got something on my face? But before I can ask, Kaidan's eyes dart back to the table and he's mumbling an excuse to leave.

I slump in my chair. He's so confusing. I'm so confused. How can I have such strong feelings for someone who cares so little about me?

Most likely because you want what you can't have. And I most definitely cannot have Kaidan. Hence, I want him. Oh so so so badly.

I angrily stand up and put my plate in the dishwasher. I do not want to go to school in the slightest because I would have to face Lucas, and the last time I saw him, he told me that he was going to make my life a living hell. Same thing with Pete, last time I saw him we were kissing and I am not ready to meet him again.

It's funny how quickly some things change.

I rush upstairs to gather everything together and clean my teeth. And that's when I see it. Kaidan's door—it's slightly open.

And he's getting changed.

Holy moley with some guacamole.

I inch towards the door slightly, like the weirdo I am and I see his reflection. Sweet Jesus, he's taking his top off.

Okay Grace, stop being weird. My subconscious hisses at me. The band of cheerleaders thinks differently, however. They're cheering me on. Hell, they're telling me to go in there and undress him myself.

No, that is too much.

His eyes suddenly see me in the reflection and my eyes widen in shock. Oh no, I look like a stalker. Abort plan! But I'm frozen in place. He's still looking at me, shirtless and confused.

Grace, for the love of God, move yourself!

I rush into my room and slam the door shut. Yep, he definitely saw me. Maybe I really am a mental patient. Seeing that I have a couple of minutes before I need to leave school, I decide to read the book Kaidan gave me.

> *The wolf is lurking in the forest; shy and timid. Every passer by flinches and gasps in horror before running away. The wolf is from another world and no one understands him. No one gives him a chance.*
>
> *He is a ruthless killing machine, who kills everything in his way. He stops at nothing; he lives up to his stereotype. But his world changes when he stumbles across a young girl in a red hood, who makes him question everything.*

Is what the blurb reads. I have read four chapters of Kaidan's book, and I am still yet to understand what he's getting at. I have reached as far as assuming that he is the wolf and I am red riding hood. But so far in the book, all that has happened is the wolf killing people and hating everyone around him.

I'm not stupid, Kaidan, I know you're not a big fan of people.

I want to continue reading but the clock dings, telling me that it's time to go. I begrudgingly walk downstairs, then leave the house and drive to school in my beautiful new car.

*   *   *

I get to school in record time, so I'm one of the first in the homeroom. I decide to kill some time by scrolling through Instagram, but then a hand places down on my desk. I look up to meet the piercing blue eyes of Lucas Keith, causing my stomach to drop.

"Morning," he says, bearing his glistening white teeth at me. "Good weekend?" The classroom begins to fill up with more people, and I feel my nerves subside a little. He can't do anything bad in front of everyone, right? *Wrong.* My subconscious tells me. *He used to do that all the time.*

174

"Great, thanks. Yours?" I try to keep my tone chipper but I really just want to punch him in the face.

"Yeah, I spent a lot of time with my uncle." He pretends to ponder for a second. "Uncles are great, aren't they? I'd kill for another one." He cocks his head to one side and winks at me. I narrow my eyes and my stomach flips as thoughts of Jared come to mind.

"But you've got what you've got." He shrugs. "Do you have an uncle, Grace?" He gives me that picture perfect smile and I feel like my world turns upside down. He doesn't know about Jared, does he? He can't.

"I don't." My voice is staccato, attempting to stop my voice from shaking. Lucas scrunches his nose patronizingly.

"Aw, well. That's too bad." He turns away from me, before turning over his shoulder and mouthing something to me. Something that looks very much like the word Jared.

I can't stop myself. I run straight out of the classroom and rush into the bathroom. I barely make it to the toilet before I'm puking my guts out. Memories are swirling my brain, filled with Jared, Lucas, and Dan.

"Lucas!" I scream happily as my blonde-haired friend enters the room. His older brother scruffs up his hair and shoves him towards me. I engulf him in a hug.

"I haven't seen you in ages!" I enthuse, playing with the hem of my new pink dress. Mommy says I'm a big girl now, so I can come to Granddad's house by myself. It's only a couple of houses down but I still feel like a grown-up walking there by myself.

"I know. Where's your mom?" he asks, flashing me a gap-toothed grin.

"She's at home. I walked here aaaallllll by myself." I swing my arms by my side while I boast.

"I had to come with Dan. Mommy has to visit the doctors for a while until she gets better." Lucas frowns.

175

"Oh. Well at least I get to see you!" I grin. "I never know what Granddad and Dan are talking about They're always so serious."

"I know," he whispers. "I overheard Dan speaking to your granddad on the phone the other day.

"Ooo!" My eyes widen. "What were they talking about?"

"Grown-up stuff. They were talking about money and about how someone didn't pay them back. They sounded pretty angry."

"Money?" I ask, my eyes crinkling in confusion.

"They were saying a man borrowed money from them and he didn't pay it back," Lucas whispers, afraid to be overheard.

I take deep breaths to calm myself down. I knew Lucas when I was younger? Dan, the drug dealer, the man who killed my uncle, is Lucas' brother?

I realize now that I'm having a panic attack. No oxygen is coming into my lungs and I'm hyperventilating. My heart is beating so fast that it feels like it's going to explode from my chest.

I knew Lucas when I was younger. Dan killed Jared.

The thoughts in my head on repeat and I try to make sense of them.

Dan killed Jared. Dan knew Granddad.

My head begins to spin and Lucas' parting words at homecoming come back to haunt me. *I'm going to make your life a living hell.*

Well done, Lucas. Mission accomplished.

THIRTY-THREE

I think I've been in the bathroom stall for over an hour now and my breathing is finally back to normal. My first official session with my psychiatrist is supposed to be in a couple of days, but I have a feeling that I'm going to need to see him sooner.

Did Granddad know that Dan killed Jared? From my memory, it seemed like they were friends, so Granddad must know the person who killed Jared. I take a deep breath and push myself off the floor. I need fresh air and I need to go home.

I stumble out into the parking lot, gasping in the cold air. It takes me a while to spot them but when I do, it becomes blindingly obvious. Two figures, hiding behind a van, whispering to each other. I try to listen to them, but their voices are extremely low that I can't make out a word they're saying. And that's when one suddenly takes something out of his pocket and passes something small to the other. Their heads are down and they look cautious. At first, I wonder why they're looking so shady but then I realize that I'm witnessing a drug deal. What kind of idiots does a drug deal on school property? Someone who clearly wants to get expelled. But then my heart rate increases when I remember the drug deal I saw between Dan and Kyle. Is one of the figures Dan? I narrow my eyes to try to distinguish who it is and when I realize, I curse myself for being so stupid. It's Lucas. His head turns and his eyes meet mine. Crap! He's seen me. I turn my head away from him so quickly that something pulls in my neck. I need to play it cool, pretend I didn't see anything. Pretend I don't know anything about Jared.

"What are you doing out here?" Lucas calls as he approaches me, turning my blood to ice. I run my shaky hands through my hair and shake my head.

"I, um, I don't feel well. I have to go home." I put my head down and try to walk towards my car. Lucas stops me, though, placing his arm out in front of me. I look up in terror and see that his face is dark.

"I know you saw that," he grinds his teeth, "and don't lie." I shake my head at him furiously, tears springing to my eyes.

Please just let me go. "I didn't see anything." Tears begin to leak down my face and I suddenly hear Lucas let out a string of curses and I flinch. *Please don't hit me.* I find myself thinking.

"Do you know what you've done?" he yells. I step back in terror.

"What I've done?" I snap feebly. "I haven't done anything." I'm weeping now. Lucas' angry eyes show no signs of sympathy.

"It could have been fine, Grace. It would have been okay. Now you've done and seen that . . ." he mutters before cursing again and kicking a trashcan. It topples over with a loud crash. I try my best to not let my fear get the best of me.

"I don't know what you're talking about!" I cry. "I just felt unwell. I am on my way home." I want to go home. I want to see Kaidan. The thought of him causes tears to gather in my eyes once more.

"Just go," he shouts. I flinch again and tears begin to trickle down my cheeks. I'm shaking and terrified. I run to my car and climb in shakily. Lucas is pacing the car park, punching walls and cursing still.

I miss the keyhole several times before I get it in because my hands are shaking so much. I pull out of the parking lot quickly and zoom home.

I stumble into the kitchen and I assume everyone is already in bed. It's late and I'm a mess. My legs collapse from underneath me and I let the tears I kept in roll down my face. Sobs rack through my body.

I hate Lucas Keith. Even more than I did when I was fat. He has some sort of association with Jared's death and I won't stop until I figure out what it is.

I suddenly hear footsteps and I look up to see Kaidan's concerned face. I don't ask why he's not at work. I don't even care what he thinks about me anymore. He can hate me all he wants but in this moment, I need him. I stand up and launch myself into his arms.

His body is tense and I can tell he's shocked. I cry into his shoulder and tighten my arms around him. *Please hug me back, Kaidan.*

My wish is his command when he circles his arms around me and rests his head on top of mine. "It's okay, Gracie."

I don't say anything, for the fear of it coming out sounding like a strangled cat. I merely shake my head in despair and continue soaking his t-shirt with my tears. My heart is still racing from the confrontation with Lucas in the parking lot. How is he related to Jared's death?

"What happened?" Kaidan says quietly as if worried to scare me off. I shake my head, because I don't want to talk about it. Because if I talk about it, it will become more real. And that terrifies me.

"It doesn't matter," I mumble into his wet shirt. I feel him nod, and silence falls between us. I finally release him and wipe the tears from my eyes.

"Gracie, you can talk to me about it. If you want," he says awkwardly, and his words cause a sudden surge of anger to rush through me. Why does he do this? One moment he acts like he hates me and the other he acts like he actually cares. It doesn't make sense.

179

"I would if you'd let me be your friend," the words come out of my mouth sharply.

"What?"

"Your mood is so changeable, Kaidan. I can't keep up. One minute you act like we're friends and another you don't. It messes with my head." I tell him, my voice still shaky. "Sometimes, I even think you hate me."

"Why do you want to be friends with someone who you think hates you?" he says bluntly. I don't know what comes over me. I really don't. The anger at Kaidan, the terrifying idea that Lucas played a role in Jared's murder, the amnesia, it all culminates into a tidal wave of emotion and the words come out before I can stop them.

"Because, Kaidan," I'm stumbling, stuttering, trying to find words to say. "I'm in love with you!" It slips out amongst my rage. Oh no.

He stills, and horror fills his eyes. Tears are still rolling down my cheeks and the look on his face makes me realize my confession was a bad move.

"No, you don't, Grace," he mumbles and the use of my actual name makes my stomach sink. Oh no. What have I done? My eyes are darting all over the place. Anywhere, everywhere but him.

"It doesn't matter," I grumble. "I'll just, er, go to, um, my room."

His face is hard and he looks angry. "You don't love me. You don't know what you're talking about."

Tears of sadness are now rolling down my cheeks as the tidal wave of emotion runs over me. I shake my head, unsure of what to say. I finally meet his unforgiving eyes.

"I guess I was right then," he says coldly. "The prissy teenage girl fell in love with the bad boy after all." He smirks. My stomach turns over and I feel sick. How could he? After seeing me

180

crying, then declaring my love for him, he decides to be horrible to me?

A solitary tear runs down my cheek and I take a deep breath. Adrenaline courses through my body and before I can stop myself, I bring my hand up and slap him hard.

*   *   *

I'm in my room, crying my eyes out. I've had the worst day on record. Just when I thought Kaidan was becoming nice again, he says that.

Yet I still can't stop falling for him.

Why am I so naïve and stupid? Why would I think that declaring my love for him would be a good idea?

Over the past week, my feelings have been on a rollercoaster and I hate that Kaidan has that power over me.

Every so often I hear a thump from Kaidan's room. It sounds like he's punching something. Has my confession made him that angry?

Tears continue down my cheeks and I feel terrible. My throat is sore and my eyes feel like they're on fire. In hindsight, I should have realized that Kaidan's reaction would have been like that.

I eye The Wolf Book on the table and throw it across the other side of the room. Why give me a birthday present if you hate me so much?

I suddenly see a piece of paper fall out of the book and my curiosity gets the best of me. I wander over to see the book open on a certain page whose page number is circled in black pen. The note says nothing on it except my name. I vaguely wonder if it's a bookmark before casting my eyes over the pages.

And through the forest, the wolf had grown to not hate little
red. In fact, his feelings for her had grown. But she is fragile, she is

perfect, she is wonderful. And the wolf does not deserve someone like her.

She became the light of his life, making him have a different perspective over the world. But they could not be together and he knew that.

She was the light, and he was the darkness. They were from completely different worlds. Hers was serene, full of tranquility. He lived in the dark. He was not right for her.

And as his feelings grew and grew for her, he realized that she felt the same way. But she was naïve. She had no idea.

The only way to stop her from her growing feelings was to return to his old ways. Returning to being the ruthless, killing machine so she can't see his true colors, hiding his true self and the fact that he had fallen head over heels in love with her.

My mouth has fallen open. What is Kaidan trying to tell me? Is he trying to tell me that the reason he acts the way he does is because . . . he has feelings for me? That he's in love with me?

He can't . . . not the way he treats me.

He can't be insinuating I'm perfect. He is right for me. He needs to realize that.

I close the book and storm over to his room but when I get there, I see all his stuff has gone. My stomach drops.

He's left.

THIRTY-FOUR

I'm going to see my psychiatrist. I need him to explain and help me comprehend what is going on. As I make my way into the kitchen, I see Dad on the phone.

"Kaidan, listen to me, you have such potential," he murmurs. My breath catches in my throat. I can't let Dad know it was my fault he left, so I run out of the door. I drive as quickly as I can to the hospital and race to the psychiatric wing.

"Grace Connely?" I say to the receptionist. She nods and gives me directions to Dr. Handon's room. He greets me with a big smile and gestures to the seat opposite him.

"A little earlier than our scheduled time, Grace. Is everything okay?" he asks me in that soothing tone of his. I take a deep breath.

"I've regained more memories." As the words tumble from my mouth, my heart beats faster and faster. "And they're not good." My eyes fill with tears and I place my head in my hands.

"Are these memories regarding your uncle? Are they distressing?" Dr. Hanson asks with a steady tone. I nod and take another deep breath.

"My former bully . . . he . . . I used to know him when I was younger." I manage. I exhaled after 3 counts and inhaled still counting to three. "His brother is named Dan. Dan killed my uncle."

"I see." Dr. Hanson looks lost for words for a moment. "I'm sure that discovery must have been heart-wrenching for you. Could you tell me the memory that led you to piece this together?"

"I was young. It must have been before Jared's murder. I went to my granddad's house. Lucas was there with his brother. Lucas and I were discussing about Granddad and Dan's business. There was something about a man who hadn't paid back some money." I explain as clearly as I can. Dr. Hanson nods.

"So, your grandfather knew the man who killed his son, correct?" he asks, and I nod. How messed up is my life?

"He isn't a bad man." I say, feeling as if I need to provide justification to Dr. Hanson. He just nods.

"I believe you. And how does it make you feel . . ." He pauses. ". . . that your grandfather knew a murderer?"

"Horrible. What do you think?" I snap unintentionally. I know he's trying to help, but his tone is coming across as extremely judgmental.

"Grace, I am trying to help you regain more memories. Discussing ones that you already remember is extremely helpful. I know it's hard, but if you want the rest of your memories back, you are going to have to talk about this. Can you do that for me?" he asks, and I nod. He's my psychiatrist. Of course, he is just trying to help.

"Let's talk about your earlier memories." He pauses. "Do you feel comfortable talking about the ones where Jared was killed?" he asks. The thought makes my stomach recoil but I nod. "Okay, Grace. When you're ready, start from the very beginning."

Here we go. "I was walking from the theatre with Jared. That's when Dan and a couple of other men surrounded us, asking for money." My stomach plummets and I look at Dr. Hanson with wide eyes. "Oh my god. Do you think that Jared was the man that Granddad and Dan were talking about in the other memory?" My breathing begins to become quicker as the memories whirl in my mind and Lucas' voice haunts me. *They were saying a man borrowed money from them, and he didn't pay it back.*

"Take some deep breaths, Grace," Dr. Hanson tells me, but I'm already spinning, falling into a black hole as another memory resurfaces.

"Granddad!" I yell as I stumble into the care home. He looks over, stands up then embraces me.

"How's my little pumpkin?" he says in that deep voice of his.

"I lost my sixth tooth today and I got a present from the tooth fairy!" I say, baring my teeth to show the gap.

"My my. Aren't you getting old?" he chuckles.

"I'm seven and three-quarters, actually." I grin and he returns it with crinkled eyes and a large smile.

"Very old." He pauses, his eyes flickering over to Dad. "I need to speak to your dad, pumpkin. But my carer, Sarah, is bringing some cakes in. Why don't you go help her?"

I nod and bound out of the room. I stop when I hear their low voices.

"Jared was killed, Dad," Dad says. "He was killed half a year ago and you didn't even show at the funeral."

"I was sick." Granddad looks away and fiddles with his ring.

"Sick? God, you weren't sick. You're not sick now! You do not need to be in a care home. You're more active and healthier than me," Dad snaps furiously. I hide behind the door, cautious of getting caught.

"I have dementia. You know that," Granddad says, then Dad curses.

"That's a lie. You have dissociative amnesia and that was in the past. Don't try that bullshit with me." Dad seethes. Granddad goes silent.

"It was my fault," Granddad mumbles.

"What? What was your fault?" Dad hisses.

"Jared's death. It was my fault."

"Deep breaths, Grace," Dr. Hanson's voice is groggy as the memory plays in my mind over and over. How can Jared's death be Granddads' fault? I saw it. I saw Dan shoot him.

"Grace, take some breaths," his voice is calming and he eventually comes back into my field of awareness. I take a couple of deep breaths, feeling the cold air stream to the back of my throat as I attempt to calm myself down.

"He played a part . . ." My voice breaks halfway through the sentence. "He played a part in Jared's death."

"Who did, Grace, your grandfather?" he asks, careful with his words as usual. I nod and place my head in my hands as tears rise to the surface. "I see." He knows not to say anything else because I have nothing else to say to him. I don't know how Granddad played a role in Jared's death and I need to know.

"I have to go," I say abruptly, wiping my face to clear it from tears. Dr. Hanson frowns at me and glances at the clock.

"We still have a lot of time left. Are you sure?" he responds, but I shake my head.

"I have to go. I'll see you on our next session." I don't wait for his reply and hurry out of his room.

*   *   *

I'm home in record time. I need to confront my grandfather. I don't care if I'm going to trigger him to have an episode. I just really need to talk to him. He said that most of his memories are back. So, he should be able to explain things to me in detail. My hands are shaking as I enter his number on my phone. He answers on the third ring.

"Hello Grace," he says warmly.

"Granddad," I say, trying to keep my voice easy. "I know I can be a trigger for you but I need some explanation."

"I thought I would be hearing from you soon. I take it you're ringing to ask about your uncle," he says calmly. How can he be so calm?

"Surprisingly enough, yes!" I snap. Good thing no one is home. "I regained a memory. One where you were talking business

186

with Dan, the man who killed Jared. So, please explain to me why you were liaising with the man who killed your son!" My voice has risen to a shout as anger courses through me.

"Grace, hear me out. It is an awful story but you need to understand. I didn't mean for any of it to happen," he says.

"No explanation justifies killing your own son!" I'm fuming now. I hear him sigh on the other side of the phone. I know I'm being unreasonable, but the anger igniting through my veins is talking for me.

"Just listen," he says with that remarkably calm voice again.

"Fine," I snap.

"My parents left me when I was sixteen. I was basically homeless and getting a job wasn't easy. Then one time, I got mugged by a gang. When I fought back, I spiked their interest and offered me everything I could ask for—a roof over my head, food, and money. Without thinking twice, I took up their proposition."

I interrupt, "I assume this was the gang that killed Jared."

"Yes. Just listen. Please don't interrupt," he says. I want to snap back telling him he shouldn't be the one giving conditions but I want to know everything, so I keep my mouth shut.

"As years passed, the gang became more prominent, recruiting people all the time. My role rose in the hierarchy and in no time, I became the leader. I know it is bad to be in a gang, but it was my only way to support my family.

"The gang eventually grew that I barely knew anyone. The only people I was in contact with were those high up. They kept me informed about our business and I made decisions.

"When I grew older, I had even less to do with it. A younger, fresher member helped me in my decision-making. Dan Keith."

My stomach drops at the mention of Dan. Granddad continues.

"He was only eighteen at that time but he was already very influential. I didn't want to be so involved anymore, but I still needed money for my family.

"I heard through the grapevine that someone had borrowed an amount of money and hadn't paid back. As a one-off comment, I simply told Dan to do what he needed to get it back. I had no idea that that man was my own son.

"When I was the leader, we never once killed anyone. But Dan killed Jared. And when I found out . . . I dropped everything. I took all the money and lost all contact with them.

"I came to the care home to deal with my amnesia. The reason I experienced it was the same reason as you, Grace. I was traumatized by the idea that I was partly responsible for Jared's death," he finishes.

I take a deep breath, absorbing all the information he gave me. "Were you involved in the drug dealing?" I say sharply.

"When I was part of the gang, drugs were involved, yes. That was the way we made money." His voice sounds weak, embarrassed. He should be. "But the drugs we dealt were class B or lower."

As if that justifies it, I want to say. But I let him continue.

"The gang is still very much alive with Dan ruling, bringing in millions of dollars from drug dealing. Drugs you haven't even heard of. Drugs so dangerous that they can't even be classified as class A." I hear him take a sharp intake of breath.

"Okay," I say slowly, my voice full of confusion.

"Grace, you have to know that Jared's death was the worst moment of my life. I regret ever joining that gang and staying with them for such a long time. I am so sorry."

"It's okay," I choke, unsure of what to say. I disapprove, but there isn't much else I can do. I have fit together the puzzle pieces now. And that's what I wanted.

"I love you very much, darling. I hope you don't hate me," he says warmly, and I sigh.

"Of course, I don't hate you. I just wish I had known." A tear falls and I silently wonder if my tear ducts are going to run dry soon.

We bid our goodbyes before I hang up. I collapse on my bed and that's when I hear the door creak open downstairs.

THIRTY-FIVE

Will is at the gym. Dad is at work. Mom is at the studio. Is Kaidan back?

I rush downstairs immediately and my stomach drops when I see Lucas standing by the table. His face is stony and his eyes are narrowed. My stomach feels hollow and my heart beats like it would come out of my chest.

"What are you doing here, Lucas?" I say, trying to keep my voice steady. All I can think of is his brother. His brother killed my uncle.

"To make amends, Grace." Something glistens in his eyes, and I feel sick. "But first, a drink? You sound parched."

I narrow my eyes. "Get out of my house, Lucas."

"We need to talk about the incident in the parking lot," he sneers, rounding the table so he's closer to me. Nerves rack through my body. *I'm going to make your life a living hell.*

"There is nothing to discuss," I say, trying to keep my voice stable. "I didn't see anything."

Lucas shuffles around the table so we're now next to each other. I stand my ground.

"You cannot tell anyone, Grace. I will leave you alone, just don't tell anyone," he says slowly and he almost sounds vulnerable. His hand moves to my arm. I flinch away from him but he holds me tight.

190

"Are you going to tell anyone?" he murmurs. His grip on my arm tightens, hurting me. I let out a small whimper.

"Get off me," I hiss, pushing him off me.

"Wrong answer," he snaps before taking something out of his pocket. I can't see what it is, causing dread to pool into my stomach. "I would have done this in the parking lot if people hadn't been around." He lifts what he's holding and my eyes widen when I see a syringe with a large needle on its end.

Oh my god.

"Lucas!" I scream, before wriggling in his tight grip. But he has a strong hold of me, his fingers surely leaving marks, digging into my skin.

I feel a harsh prick into my arm and liquid flows through me. My world starts becoming fuzzy. I try to say something but my muscles aren't responding. My limbs feel heavy and my eyes begin to roll backwards.

I feel my legs collapse from underneath me and the world fades out.

*   *   *

I'm in a car. Everything is still fuzzy. My hands are tied behind my back and a cloth is placed in my mouth preventing me to utter a word. Lucas is kidnapping me. Oh my god. Terror runs through my veins. He's going to kill me. I feel my tears arises, but nothing comes out. I feel like he has paralyzed me.

Panic runs through me. I try to move, speak, anything to get myself out of this mess. Why is he doing this? Surely, he can't be doing these extreme, definitely criminal lengths just to stop me from going to the cops.

Is this about Jared?

Oh god, everything links back to Jared.

I'm suddenly finding it hard to breath. My chest constricts and I feel like my lungs have collapsed. My last feeling is of pain and horror as I slip back into the world of nothingness again.

*   *   *

I'm groggy. Someone has their arm around me, holding me tight. It's harsh and . . . they're dragging me. My feet are scraping against the floor and my head is lolling. I have no control. I can see glass everywhere. Glass walls, desks . . . They look expensive. Granddad's words come back to me. *The gang is still very much alive with Dan ruling, bringing in millions of dollars from drug dealing."* This must be their . . . compound?

I don't know how long I've been out but it's dark outside so my guess is that it took us several hours in the car. I try to hold my head up but I'm too weak. I can't move. Voices around me are muffled and my head hurts like a bitch.

No one is going to find me here.

I'm going to die. A wave of sadness sweeps over me. I am useless. I cannot move nor speak. My body has been monopolized by whatever drug Lucas gave me.

Lucas. That son of a bitch. My body is sweating excessively and I'm granted a bit of movement as my body convulses and I throw up. My eyes are far back and my head is limp. I hear yelling around me. Another jab in my arm and my world fades once more.

*   *   *

I'm awake again, and I hear a clatter of keys. The glass is gone and the walls surrounding me are white. Someone is still holding me up with a steady arm. All I can smell is my vomit. It's all over me. I want to cry but I can't. A door swings open and loud voices struck my ears, causing my head to ache. Please. Make the

192

voices go away. And they do, as the person holding me up shoves me onto the floor with a forceful push.

THIRTY-SIX

My own snore wakes me up. I open my eyes and found myself lying on a cold floor. *And I can move.* The sensation of my hands is back and I use this new-found freedom to push myself up and look around.

My head . . . is pounding.

I'm in a small white room. There is nothing in here except a loo and a sink. It's like a prison cell.

I feel like a prisoner.

I am a prisoner.

What has Lucas done?

I laugh when I see a pile of clothes on the floor. Clean clothes. All black. These creeps. No bed, but I have clothes.

I am about to shove them through the tiny flap in the door but then I realize my own clothes stink. The thought brings up memories and I barely get to the loo before throwing up once more.

I hold myself over the sink and wash myself then gulp down some water. My body has been severely messed by that drug.

If I see Lucas again, I am going to kill him.

I strip off my clothes and hurriedly pull on the ones provided. It's a pair of black leggings and a long-sleeved black top. The fact that they got the right size causes panic to rise in me.

My head is still feeling extraordinarily light. Those drugs are really strong. I sit on the floor, feeling pain all over my body.

Rubbing my head, I eye the door. It looks secure—too secure for me to attempt to break out. A thought pops into my head and I quickly shuffle over to the flap in the door. I assume it is where they would hand out food.

The idea makes me feel sick and claustrophobic. I push the small flap to see a long white corridor. It appears that I am right at the end of a corridor. But from what I can see, there are no other rooms.

It is just me.

Are they going to leave me here to rot?

The disgusting thought is quickly removed when I see the door at the end open and someone is walking towards my room. Panic erupts in me so I quickly lie on the floor, pretending to be unconscious. Thinking that maybe they won't drug me again. The door creaks open and I hear footsteps towards me. I sense there are two people. I try to maintain my calm and keep my breathing normal. I cannot let them know I'm awake.

"So, this is the little brat?" says a voice I don't recognize.

"The very one. Thomas Connely's brat of a granddaughter," says a familiar voice. My blood runs cold. Oh, I know that drawl. It's Dan.

"So, you just want me to check her, feed her, the standard?" the unfamiliar man says. He sounds young and cruel. *The standard.* Have they done this before?

"Feed her once a day. If she gets too active, drug her again. I'm sending that photo to the Connelys tonight. I'll make sure Thomas gets a copy," Dan says. What? What photo? And why is Granddad involved?

"How much are you asking for?" says the unfamiliar voice. Oh god, they're asking for money. Am I being held for ransom? I feel sick.

"Five million dollars. He better care about this little brat enough. I want my revenge on that bastard," Dan snarls. Then I suddenly feel his boot kick forcefully into my ribs. Pain shoots through my side like fireworks and I fight tears away. That hurts.

"Let's just hope he will," says the unfamiliar man, slamming the door behind them. I gasp after a minute or so after making sure they're gone.

I sit up and grasp my side in agony. He must have broken my ribs. The pain is causing me to see stars so I lie down on my good side.

I hate him. I hate Lucas. Why are they holding me for ransom? Why do they want revenge on Granddad? He made this gang into what it is. I hope the police finds me before Granddad lets them get away with kidnapping.

*   *   *

Hours have gone by. Time has turned to nothing. I'm so hungry I can't think straight. A large bruise appears on my rib area and I feel that something is really broken. It's difficult to stand and going to the loo is an impossible task.

I won't be able to sleep here. Not on this cold, hard floor with unpleasant thoughts circulating my mind.

I can't believe that this is happening. It's something out from a movie, not in real life. Kidnapping is not something I should have to worry about but I should have been cautious and more vigilant. After all, Lucas did promise me he'd make my life a living hell.

My thoughts are interrupted when I hear the door flap open, and a tray is pushed through. It has a plate of disgusting looking food, but I'm so hungry I could eat anything. I finish the food in seconds but my stomach is still complaining. I am going to waste away into nothing.

Everything is silent. I cannot hear faded voices from outside or slamming doors. Maybe I can attempt to escape. The thought is welcome. Now's the time to do it. If I get caught, there's nothing they can do to me that's worse than what they have already done.

Except death.

I push that thought from my brain. I mustn't think like that. I will be saved. I will be.

I stand slowly, wincing before walking to the door. This doesn't look locked. I push it, and I'm surprised to see that it is open. Hmm. How bizarre. I creep along this long, white corridor before reaching the end door. Befuddlement grips me. Why isn't the security higher? I peek through the glass on the door to see a large room with a circular table in the center. What is this place?

I push the door but this one is locked. I give it a harder push, but it didn't budge. I am not giving up.

The nerdy girl within me analyzes the door, watching all those spy movies will not go to waste. The lock looks pretty standard so I'm guessing they didn't want to invest in a high security system.

I peek through the keyhole to see if there is a key on the other side. Yes, there is. My band of cheerleaders has returned and they're cautiously cheering on the sidelines. I move as quickly as my body allows me to go back to my prison room. I find some loo paper. That will do.

I return to the door and slide as much loo roll as I can into the crack under the door. I'm lucky enough that the crack is wide enough for the key.

Reaching for the clip in my hair, I push it through the hole, causing the key to fall onto the floor and onto my loo roll.

I give the loo paper a quick tug, and the key is brought with it. I rejoice. I need to be quick.

I unlock the door and push it open as quietly as I can, moving carefully into the next room. There are two doors at the back of the room.

Oh god, which one is the right one?

I creep over to the nearest one and peek through the glass part. Everything is abandoned and I see another white room which is completely empty. I silently move to the next door to see a grey corridor. I bet that leads somewhere.

I find that this door is unlocked and my subconscious is firmly telling me that there is something very off about the fact that no one is around and nothing is locked.

Creeping down the grey corridor, I'm met with another door. I push it open to see a small room with Lucas Keith standing in the middle of it.

THIRTY-SEVEN

My stomach drops. I should have known.

I keep my breathing steady and look at him. His face is soft, unlike how it was yesterday or whatever day I was kidnapped.

"I hate you," slips out of my mouth.

"I assumed as much," Lucas says, but there is no cocky smirk. What is going on? "But we need to talk."

"I have nothing to say to you, you worthless piece of scum," I hiss, making him wince.

"Sit down, Grace. Come on. I know you haven't been able to rest. Just sit, please," he begs. I narrow my eyes and comply but only because my ribs are causing pain again.

"I knew you'd figure out how to escape," Lucas murmurs. "You're motivated. Feisty. I like that about you."

"It's not exactly hard when all the doors are unlocked," I snap, ignoring his appreciative remarks.

"I did that on purpose. I've been checking on you and I know about your ribs," he says. I frown in confusion. He hasn't checked on me . . . Oh no. Do they have cameras?

"Have you been watching me through a camera?" I say with pure shock. Lucas shakes his head.

"You haven't realized. There are sedatives in your food. You've been fading in and out for days," Lucas mumbles, looking embarrassed. My stomach drops. How have I not realized?

"How long have I been here?" I croak. Lucas looks down.

"Nearly a week," he hesitates. "We've been feeding you through tubes."

I cover my mouth. My parents. Oh god, they must be thinking I'm dead.

"How could you do this?" I hiss. "Why?"

"That's why I got you here. Dan has given me an hour, max." He hesitates and takes my silence as obliging.

"Do you know about your grandfather and his role in the gang?" he asks. I nod. "Dan loved and respected him. He made our lives turn around after my mom died. He saved us.

"But when he found out about Dan killing Jared, he was beyond angry. He took all the money and left us homeless. We had nothing. Dan had to provide for me. We could barely feed ourselves. This went on for several years.

"Dan swore to get revenge on him when he could. He hates what he did to us. I hate what he did to us." Revenge. The idea makes me feel sick.

"He killed his son," I spit. "What do you expect?"

"Dan did what he needed to do." His eyes darken. "Over the summer, Dan discovered that you were Thomas Connely's granddaughter. Thomas used a fake name in the gang, you see. But Dan eventually worked it out and when he realized that you and I went to the same school? He made his plan to hold you ransom as a revenge on Thomas.

"And you timed it so well! You coming back to school looking like a model made it so easy for me. I didn't change my mind about you because I fancied you, Grace. It was just my role in the revenge plan." Bile rises in my throat. It was never about the looks for him. It was about revenge.

"My role was to get close to you. Close enough that I could get you here. But getting close to you . . . was hard. You were so stubborn and you seemed to have your own little plan, didn't you?" I don't say anything, I'm just in shock. All this time I thought that

Lucas is shallow when in reality . . . he is into something deeper. We both have our own revenge plans.

"Halloween was the night I was supposed to drug you. I was going to, after that game of beer pong with Pete. But again, you were too stubborn. You were gone in an instant. I underestimated you."

"I had friends at that party. You would've been caught," I seethe. Lucas shrugs as if agreeing with me.

"You're right. I tried to persuade Dan away from his plan, telling him that we would get caught, but he wouldn't listen. He was so caught up in his revenge plan that he was blinded.

"My last attempt was homecoming." He cocks his head to one side. "Any other girl would have killed for the chance to go to homecoming with me. But you?" He chuckles. "You decided to go with someone else."

"You're sick," I spit at him and he just shrugs again.

"I had to do what I had to do. I even nominated you for homecoming queen." He laughs and rolls his eyes. "I guess that turned out well."

"I guess so." I gulp.

"When you saw me dealing in the parking lot, I knew I had to do it. You found out too much, and if Dan knew . . . he would have probably killed you." He pauses. "I'm not a bad guy, Grace." I manage a laugh and he sighs.

"I don't like you but I don't believe in murder."

I nod and let tears run down my cheeks. "Please help me get out, Lucas." I weep. "I will believe you if you help me."

"Grace, I can't."

"Please," I whimper and I feel completely and utterly powerless. Lucas shakes his head.

"Our hour is up. Back to the cell." He takes my arm and supports me on the side where I'm not bruised.

"They're going to stop drugging your food now," he whispers into my ear, and slips two pills into my hand. "They're

201

painkillers. I promise they're not the same drugs they're giving you, trust me. I can see how much pain you're in."

I nod and put the pills into my pocket. I hope he's telling the truth. We reach my cell and he helps me sit. My mind spins because Lucas, the boy who hates me, seems to be my only ally in this situation. Who would've thought, huh?

"Your grandfather is getting the money, Grace. You're going to get out," Lucas says quietly as if he's afraid to be heard. "It'll just take time."

"It's not about the money." I mumble. "I want Dan to go to prison. He deserves it."

Lucas winces. "I know he's a bad person. But he is my brother." With that, he slams the door shut.

*   *   *

I don't know how long I've been here. Days have blurred together. I have barely slept. I've been eating the food, hoping Lucas has been taking the sedatives out.

No one has visited me. I guess that is a good sign since the one time I have been visited, my ribs got broken.

I reckon I've been here for a total of three weeks now. The days drag on and my hope is diminishing every day. My granddad doesn't have five million dollars hanging around. He won't be able to pay the ransom.

I idly wonder if my parents know.

Is there a search warrant? Where am I? It must be a very secret location if they can't still find me. Or they probably think I am dead. I dread to think what the headlines are. *Crazy girl, missing. Mental patient, dead.*

I haven't cried since my conversation with Lucas. Why can't he see clarity and help me escape? Then, he won't be arrested. But I bet they won't get caught.

I am trapped here and no one is going to find me. I have lost even more weight. One meal a day is not sufficient. My legs look like twigs and my arms feel too light.

I am wasting away.

THIRTY-EIGHT

It's been even longer. Four weeks now. Maybe five. I have lost hope. I awake from my ten-minute sleep, taking me to a world far from here.

The door opens. I'm stunned to see Dan. He looks angry.

"Why won't your grandfather pay?" he yells, then takes his leg back and gives me an almighty kick. I yelp and pain runs through me. He kicks me again. And again. And again. I begin to see stars and a single thought crosses my foggy brain.

He's going to kill me. "Leave me alone, please," I whimper.

"No," he snarls, before bending down and pulling me up harshly. He pulls his phone out of his pocket and dials a number. "Hello Thomas."

Granddad. Oh no. What is he going to do?

"It's good to hear from you. Have you got my money?" Dan says. "Wait, I'll put you on speakerphone so you can chat with your brat of a granddaughter."

"Grace?" It's Granddad. He sounds weak.

"Don't pay them. They're ass—" I start, but Dan shuts me up by slapping me harshly across the cheek.

"Don't hurt her!" Granddad yells down the phone. Dan laughs.

"I won't need to, if you just give me the money," Dan drawls.

"Dan, I only have three million. Just take it and give me my granddaughter back," Granddad says. Three million? I didn't know he had that much money.

"A deal's a deal. Get me five million," Dan says.

"It is physically impossible, Dan. And if you lay a finger on Grace, you will get none of it."

"Old man, you are no match for me. You get the money, or I'll beat her up so badly that you won't have a granddaughter anymore," Dan snarls. My heart starts to best in panic and I don't know what to do.

"I gave you so much. I saved you. Remember how much I cared about you," Granddad frets, and I can tell he's groveling now. Anything to save me.

"If you cared about me, then why did you take all the money and basically leave us for dead!" Dan yells down the phone.

"You killed my son!" Granddad yells back.

No, don't shout. Don't make Dan even angrier.

"You told me to! You told me to do what was needed to get the money!" Dan spits. "And he didn't have it, so we killed him."

"I never meant kill. You knew me well enough to know that," Granddad hisses. Dan's grip loosens a little on my shirt. Maybe I should punch him when he isn't expecting it. But I'm so weak. My ribs are severely bruised and I'm pretty sure they still put sedatives in my food.

"He borrowed too much. He had to be killed," Dan hisses.

Adrenaline rushes through me as he says those hateful words and I bring my hand up and punch him in the face hard. Clearly he is taken by surprise and his phone falls out of his hand, making him release his hold on my shirt. Ow, that hurt my hand. He is still in a daze, so I quickly bring up my leg and kick him in the balls. *You deserve this, you son of a bitch.*

He falls down onto his knees shouting out in pain. "You little brat!"

205

I run as fast as I can. But when I hear him running behind me, I know I won't get far. His hands reach my waist and pushes me onto the floor.

I slam onto the hard surface hitting my chin with an impact, blood immediately oozing out. I cry out in pain before Dan drags me back to my cell.

"Don't ever do that again," he hisses. He picks up his phone.

"You've got a feisty one," Dan snarls.

"If you hurt her . . ." Granddad says quietly but anger is clear in his voice.

"Too late. Bring me my money or else I'll give you a little preview of what will happen to her if you don't."

"No!" I yell, before he brings his fist backwards and punches my face. Pain bursts on my cheekbones and I begin to feel dizzy. He grabs me by the hair and yanks, making me scream out in pain.

I think Granddad is shouting at him to stop but I can hear nothing through the pain.

Dan shoves me onto the floor and my head hits the hard surface. I'm going to pass out. Everything in my body is in pain. I'm screaming as he kicks my ribs, my legs, and my face.

I scream and scream before I blackout from the pain.

*　　*　　*

I'm woken up by the sound of voices. "Oh Gracie," one says, caressing my face. No, that hurts. I find it hard to open my eyes. Am I dreaming?

Someone is carrying me. They are firm and warm opposite to how cold my body is. Everything hurts.

"Is she alive?" says a voice. Will? Is that Will? I must be dreaming.

"Yes. Dan beat her up really badly though. The second I heard, I lost it. The cops will be here soon." Is that Lucas? The cops? I am so confused.

I fade back out. The pain in my ribs is pulling me into unconsciousness.

When I wake up, I am still being carried. They're trying to be as careful as possible but every movement is causing bursts of pain throughout my entire body.

"How close is the hospital?" I hear from an Australian sounding voice. My heart skips a beat. Kaidan? Kaidan is carrying me. Oh, please be real. Please. Using the little strength I have, I fist his shirt. I want him to know I'm here with them.

"She's moving!" Kaidan says with a relieved tone. *See, Big Bad Wolf. You care about me after all.*

"Grace, can you hear us?" It's Will again. We're still moving quickly. I try to move my head but I' too weak. Dammit.

"If you can, you're okay. Lucas helped us get you out. We're going to the hospital now. It's going to be okay," Will says soothingly. I wish I could respond.

And Lucas. He helped them. Oh, this is all so confusing. My head begins to throb, and I feel a tear escape from my eye.

I fade back into nothingness.

*   *   *

I feel something in my arm. I don't know what. My head is still heavy and I cannot open my eyes. But I am lying on a bed.

"Will she be awake soon?" Kaidan says. He's here. I just want to be able to see him. To tell him how much I missed him. To tell him that I love him.

"I don't know. She still has an awful lot of the drug they used in her system. It's unknown to us, so we do not know its effects," the nurse says.

"Can she hear me?" he asks.

207

Yes! Kaidan, I can hear you!

"I couldn't tell. She might be able to, but she won't be able to respond." I hear footsteps and then the nurse has left the room.

"Gracie . . ." he mumbles, before taking my hand in his. "I hope you can hear me."

I can, Kaidan.

"I am so sorry for everything. I . . . I was so horrible." His voice cracks. "I hurt you so much. And that is why I am not right for you. I wish I were. Seeing you on that floor so vulnerable made me realize how close I was to losing you." He's crying. "If I ever lost you . . . I would never recover."

My heart breaks. He cares. Oh, how much he cares. I wish I could just wake up and kiss him. But I can't.

"I'm so sorry for kissing you. I couldn't help myself. But then I realized it was a wrong move. I was just trying to stop you from developing feelings for me. I thought that if you stopped liking me, I could stop liking you."

Everything inside me lights up. I am so in love with him. I just want to be with him and tell him I feel exactly the same way.

"But I am in love with you. So that makes things more difficult," I hear him chuckle to himself.

An unstoppable smile reaches my lips. *I can move.*

"Gracie?"

I tilt my head forwards, attempting to nod before opening my eyes. I know my face is wholly bruised, probably explaining why I'm finding it difficult to do anything. I see Kaidan sitting by my bed, his hand in mine. His eyes are red and he looks exhausted. How long have I been out?

"Kaidan," I croak, my voice is hoarse and whispery. He chuckles and gives me a breathtaking smile.

"I suppose you heard all of that, then," he says, with a small blush reaching his cheeks.

"Maybe," I say shyly. I bet I'm looking lovely now.

208

"You don't look surprised," he mumbles, before kissing my knuckles.

"I finished the book you gave me." I give him a small smile. "It made everything so much clearer."

"I should have never left . . . if I'd stayed . . . " Kaidan says guiltily.

"Dan was going to stop at nothing." I shudder at the thought. "Is he . . . ?"

"He's been arrested." Kaidan seethes. "If I could get my hands on him, I swear to God . . ."

"And Lucas?" I don't know what I feel about Lucas. He deserves to go to prison but he helped get me out.

"Lucas was the one who saved you. But . . ." Kaidan sighs, "he's been arrested, too. He might get away with a shorter sentence for helping you out and complying with the detectives." He shrugs. "I don't know."

I nod.

"I was so worried, Gracie."

"Why? Why would Lucas do that, turn against his brother knowing that he'd be arrested too?"

Kaidan closes his eyes as if scared to tell me. "He told us that Dan was planning on killing you. Your grandfather didn't have the money." I feel my stomach drops. He was going to kill me? "Lucas said that he couldn't let that happen. He said he'd rather be in prison than live with the guilt of your death on his hands." His voice cracks. "I'm so sorry, Gracie."

"I'm fine now, Kaidan. Everything is okay," I reassure him, even though I'm not sure myself. There is a thick bandage around my ribs and my face just feels like one huge bruise. I take a deep breath.

"No, it's not, Gracie. I mean look at you. You've wasted away," Kaidan says sadly, like it's his fault.

"I will be fine. What about you. Are you okay? You look exhausted."

"I'm fine. I want to stay with you until you're better," he says with love and adoration in his eyes. My cheerleaders have regained themselves and are performing an elaborate routine in my name.

"I want you to stay too," I say quietly. He smiles at me before leaning forward and placing a kiss on my forehead.

"I am so in love with you, Grace Connely."

THIRTY-NINE

It's day four in the hospital. Kaidan has only left once and that was on my request to get my body weight back in pizza.

Obviously, he joked about the fact that I didn't have any body weight, causing an angry response from me. The doctors told me I lost quite a lot of weight while I was kidnapped, putting me at a very unhealthy weight of 110 pounds.

But I guess that means I can eat as much as I want until I get to a healthy weight. Silver linings, I guess. My family have been in and out. Mom initially being a blubbering mess and Dad just showering Kaidan with thanks. My knight in shining armor.

Kaidan explained to me that Lucas had called Will, telling him what was going on. Kaidan was about to get on his flight back to Australia when he heard the news that I was missing. Apparently, they'd been searching for weeks.

My mind continues to wander to the 'what if's'. What if Lucas hadn't called Will? What if I'd been there for a week longer? I don't want to think about it because all questions lead to one answer: I would be dead by now.

Amber and Jacob have visited on multiple occasions and informed me that Lucas' uncle, the principal, was found to be involved in the gang as well. He's been put behind bars and I say good riddance.

Kaidan comes back carrying a stack of pizzas. My eyes widen in anticipation. I am so hungry. He's grinning like a little boy and he swiftly places a kiss on my lips. Oh, and I guess we're kind of a thing now. Not that he's ever kissed me properly—he's too worried he'll hurt me. But what about 'a kiss will make it feel better'? I grin at my Greek god. Mine and no one else's. Wow, I'm such a psycho. Thank god he can't read my mind.

"Pepperoni, per your request your highness." He places the pizza on my table. I clap my hands together.

"Why thank you, Kanye." I wink at him. "Or is it Kris? Kiden?" I tease and watch as his irritated expression grow.

"Just because you're in hospital doesn't mean I can't kick your ass," he says slyly. I narrow my eyes. He would never even dare.

"Kaidan, I know you well enough to know you wouldn't dare," I say with narrowed eyes. I love it when he's playful. He's adorable and he has no idea.

"You're right." He brushes his finger over my cheekbone. "Your bruise is fading."

"Thank goodness," I say. Kaidan has been seeing me looking like a wreck yet for some bizarre reason, he still wants to be with me.

"How you manage to still look good with a bruised face is beyond me," he mumbles, tucking a strand of hair behind my ear. I blush while my cheerleaders swoon. I don't know what to say, so I respond by shoving one whole slice of pizza into my mouth. Obviously, it doesn't all fit, so tomato sauce oozes out of the corners.

Kaidan is cracking up and I give him a pizza filled grin. "Hot right? I am such a lucky guy," he chuckles. He eats his pizza as well but not quite as messily as I do.

We chat generally while we eat our pizza. He fills me in on what I missed while I was away, subtly slipping in that Will and Amber have been seeing each other. I gape in surprise.

"What?" I yelp. My brother and Amber. Ew!

"Amber was at the house all the time while you were missing. They have comforted each other and now I guess they're a thing," Kaidan says nonchalantly. I guess he's good for Amber. I knew he was into her. I love conversations like this. It shows me that my life is slowly returning to normal. And I have a . . . boyfriend? Is he even my boyfriend?

"So, are they like, official?" I ask, subtly bringing it up.

"I guess," he mutters. I nod slowly.

"Oh, that's good for them," I say while not meeting his eyes. He nods slowly. He is being stupid. Am I not being obvious?

"Christ, Kaidan! Just ask me to be your girlfriend already!" I blurt out, regretting it immediately. Kaidan looks at my expression in horror before bursting out in laughter.

"Gracie," he laughs. "I didn't think it needed clarification. You are my girlfriend and no one else."

I scowl. Oh, well, at least we made that clear.

"Okay then." I eat another slice of pizza. Mmm.

"Gracie?" Kaidan asks. I look at him sideward.

"Yes," I say shortly. He's still laughing at me! This is not a laughing matter. Well, maybe it is. But I will not give him that satisfaction.

"Will you be my girlfriend?" He's trying to keep a straight face yet failing massively. I stick my tongue out at him and eat another slice of pizza. He's suddenly on his knees and he takes my hand.

"Grace Connely, I love you. Please, I beg of you, be my girlfriend," he manages to hold his laughter until the end.

I admire him as he laughs. He's so goddamn attractive. "Okay, I guess," I say nonchalantly, before taking my hand from his. He sits back down on his chair. He kisses my forehead, my cheeks, and my whole face.

"Ew! Get off me!" I shriek.

"You love it, really." He winks, before settling down and shoving a slice of pizza in his mouth.

"You're wrong," I say, folding my arms. But he's not wrong. He's completely right.

"We both know I'm not."

*   *   *

After a week, I'm finally out of the goddamn hospital. Since Kaidan hasn't left my side the entire week, he's the one to take me home. As we walk to the car, he casually takes my hand in his.

On the inside, I squeal like a little girl. It's such a small gesture, but also such an un-Kaidan thing for him to do. I grin at him and climb into the car.

I sing loudly along to Taylor Swift songs on the journey. Who can blame me? I finally have my freedom and a drool-worthy boyfriend. "I don't know about you but I'm feeling twenty-two!" I yell at the top of my lungs, causing Kaidan to wince and cover one ear.

"You sound like a strangled cat," he comments. I grin stupidly. I don't care. I feel on top of the world and no one can stop me.

I carry on singing the whole way home. When we enter the house, everyone suddenly jumps out shouting "Surprise!" I grin and look around. Everyone is here. Mom, Dad, Will, Amber, Jacob, Pete, and several other school friends. I cover my mouth in surprise and give everyone a hug.

I rush upstairs to have a quick shower so I can look presentable for the party. My bruises are yellowy now so I will be able to cover them with makeup. After my shower I dry my hair and put some makeup on to improve my appearance.

Throwing on a maroon dress, I rush back downstairs to my awaiting friends. We spend the evening eating, laughing, dancing and drinking until everyone is drunk, full and ridiculously happy. I haven't had this amazing time in forever. I savor this evening in the presence of these amazing, wonderful people that I love so dearly.

*　　*　　*

I'm exhausted and drunk. Kaidan and I flop onto my bed in hysterics. I don't even know what we're laughing at, but for some reason it's very funny.

Kaidan isn't drunk in the slightest and somehow his presence is managing to sober me up. "Last time we were here . . ." I stifle a giggle. Kaidan's face falls before stroking my cheek.

"I am so sorry," he mumbles, before rolling over and leaning over me. He kisses my cheeks, lingering on my bruises. He then finally kisses my lips. It's light and tame at first, as if he's still trying to be careful with me. So naturally, I deepen the kiss, pulling Kaidan down closer and wrap my arms around his neck. I have waited a week for this. A very long week at that.

He presses himself against me so we're even closer and I run my hands through his hair. He caresses me—my legs, stomach, face . . . and it feels incredible. I feel like we are made for each other. The way our mouths fit each other, the way his hand fits in mine.

In this moment, I am completely ready to give myself to him.

I do.

215

EPILOGUE

"Dearly beloved, we are gathered here today..."

Seven years later, Kaidan and Grace's wedding

"My Gracie," Kaidan begins, "I love you with everything in me. Everything about you makes me who I am today. Our love story isn't a typical one." He chuckles, earning a couple of laughs from the crowd. "Most do not include psychogenic amnesia, a kidnapping . . . and somehow managing to fall in love in between that mess." He grins and takes my hand. "I promise to love and care for you, and I will try in every way to be worthy of your love. I will always be honest with you, kind, patient, and forgiving. I promise to grow old with you and support you in everything that you do. But most of all, I promise to be a true and loyal friend to you. I love you."

A tear runs down my cheek. "Kaidan," I start and my voice is hoarse. "You know me better than anyone else in this world and somehow you still manage to love me. You are my best friend and one true love. There is still a part of me today that cannot believe that I'm the one who gets to marry you. I am hopelessly, incandescently and irrevocably in love with you."

Our guests applaud us and I see Mom silently crying in the front pew. Kaidan places the beautiful ring onto my finger and I place one on his, before he takes me and tips me downwards. I gasp in surprise but he silences me by kissing me on the lips. I hear the photographer clicking away and I smile into his lips.

Our reception is themed blue and everyone looks stunning. Will has Amber on his arm, who already looks drunk. I know she's keen for Will to ask for her hand but he's really taking his time. She throws herself into my arms and I support her.

Yes. Definitely drunk.

It's time to throw the bouquet. All the girls form a crowd behind me and Jacob joins them. He looks determined. I give them a cheeky smile.

"May the best woman," I say, which makes Jacob cough, "or man, win."

I then throw the bouquet behind me. I turn around to see Jacob jumping up and down victoriously. Amber is sending him evils, before stomping up to Will who is crying with laughter.

Kaidan and I wander onto the dance floor for our first dance as husband and wife. He takes me into his arms and the music starts. He holds me and his eyes bore into mine. He spins me around then holds me again in a loving dance watched by everyone.

As the music fades into a more upbeat song, everyone else joins in. It's a beautiful evening but it won't last forever. Soon enough, Kaidan and I are tipsy and in the finest hotel in Boston.

"Mrs. Micah, what a beautiful dress you're wearing," he says lowly while wandering over to me. He stands a head taller than me even with my heels on. "But I'm going to have to let you know that it would certainly look better on the floor."

I give him a sly grin and turn around so he can undo the beautiful corset. I step out of my amazing dress carefully then proceed with undoing his shirt. I gaze at my beautiful *husband*. I am one lucky girl.

*　　　*　　　*

Jacob and Javi's wedding

"I now pronounce you, man and man." The minister grins. This is the most beautiful wedding I've ever been to. I watch Jacob and Javi shyly kiss each other before walking down the aisle hand in hand. We're on the beach, all of us barefoot and the women wearing flowing dresses.

Jacob wanted it to be a relaxed wedding and so it is. I glance at Kaidan in the crowd. He's smiling at me, wearing a ridiculous tropical shirt that makes his tan appear even darker.

Only Javi's parents, Jacob's parents, Amber, Will, Kaidan, and I are here. Pete couldn't come since his wife went into labor just before we were going to take off.

Oh yes, Pete. Pete 'got over' me in grand total of about two months and met this gorgeous Italian girl who adores him. They have now been married for two years and were the first couple in our group to seal the deal.

We all wander up to the Hawaiian themed reception which is serving cocktails of all sorts. Kaidan joins me at the bar.

"Hello beautiful." He kisses me on the cheek. I grin and take his hand.

"Did you enjoy the ceremony?" I ask him.

"Oh, yes, it was amazing. I couldn't keep my eyes off you though," he tells me. He then orders himself an extravagant drink. I roll my eyes. What a cheeseball.

"Something for you, my gorgeous wife?" he asks me. Wow, this is going to be hard to get used to.

*   *   *

Amber and Will's wedding

Everything is hectic. Mad. The bridesmaids are running around like headless chickens and Amber is taking shots of vodka from her purse every five seconds.

"Amber, calm down. Seriously, it's fine," Jacob soothes.

218

"Calm down!" she shrieks. "You think I'm capable of calming down! The wedding is a mess! No one is in their places! And where on earth is Grace?"

I rush into the room as I hear my name. "Present," I huff. Amber is seriously not appreciating how much I am doing for her right now. But it is her big day, so what the bride wants, the bride gets. Jacob and I have the joint maid of honor title. It makes it so much easier with two people on the job. Plus, Kaidan being the best man to Will isn't useful since he is hopeless at organization.

"Amber, the flowers are fine and the band is already in the reception. Everything is going smoothly." I say in my calmest voice. Her eyes widen into saucepans.

"Then where is my makeup artist?!" she screeches. I resist the urge to hold my ears and look to Jacob in urgency.

"Javi will be here any moment, Ambs," Jacob says awkwardly.

"Well, your husband is hopeless! He was supposed to be here half an hour ago!" she shrieks. Javi suddenly rushes into the room and showers Amber with apologies. She immediately calms down and settles in her chair to let Jacob's beautiful husband get to work.

Amber wanted to have her wedding in New York and so she did. Plus, it's Amber, she doesn't do anything small. It's happening in the most beautiful hall and I don't even know how many guests she has. It looks amazing so I am very confused as to why she is fretting so much.

My phone buzzes and I wander to the hallway to see Kaidan standing there in his suit.

"Gracie, can you do my tie?" he asks. I quickly peck him on the lips before obliging.

"How's bump?" he asks me as I concentrate. I bump my large stomach into him. Nine months along the line, it could be any day now.

"Bump is frustrating. And painful. And making this dress look terrible," I complain, stretching my back uncomfortably.

"You look gorgeous. Just don't go into labor until the wedding is over. Amber will kill you if you steal her thunder." He's more talking to bump than he is to me. He kisses my stomach and then me, before rushing down the hallway to aid Will.

I return to find Amber fully made up. Thank God. She seems a lot calmer now.

"Okay, places!" the wedding planner shouts.

*   *   *

Will and Amber kiss after they are pronounced man and wife. I glance over to see Pete and his wife, Kira, trying to keep their little girl quiet. It seems that they are being unsuccessful. I rub my stomach. *Please be better behaved than her, bump.*

The band at the reception is great. I wish I could dance too, but bump is making me too uncomfortable.

Pete wanders over to me, leaving Kira with the now calm little girl. I give him a kiss on the cheek on greeting.

"How's fatherhood treating you?" I chuckle. He sighs and rubs his forehead.

"She's a little madam, that one."

"It's Leila, isn't it?" I ask. He nods, then gestures to bump.

"What about you? You should be due any day now, right?" he asks. I nod tiredly.

"It's so uncomfortable. I just want him to get out of me," I chuckle.

"Oh, so you found out the gender?" he asks with furrowed eyebrows.

I shake my head. "No, but I really feel like it's going to be a boy. Although I'm pretty sure Kaidan wants a girl." I laugh, glancing over to my husband who is dancing with Mom happily.

"It's so weird how much our lives have changed. Yet we're all still friends," Pete states. I nod. It is. We all still live in Boston and, as of today, we are all married.

My mind flickers back to high school, thinking of Lucas. After a court hearing, Lucas was sentenced five years in prison to pay for his part in my kidnapping. I assume he's out now, but I don't know where he is. And I'm glad.

"Anyway, I think it's my turn to look after Leila, so I better shoot off. But best wishes with labor." He winks. I give him a quick hug, being careful not to press bump to hard.

"We should all have coffee next week or something," Pete suddenly says. "It's been a while since we've all met up."

"Yes, why don't we go out for lunch?" I suggest. Pete nods eagerly before heading over to Kira and Leila. I idly wonder how his mom is getting on. I know she stopped the affair with Kyle's dad and I think she may have met a new man. I hope she's happy.

As for Kyle . . . no one has heard from him since high school. And I'm not particularly bothered that he didn't stay in touch.

I carefully sit myself down. *Oh bump, get out of me.*

Kaidan wanders over to me. "Come dance with me, Gracie."

I shake my head. "Nope. Firstly, I will look like an idiot. Secondly, it may agitate bump and make him come out." I shift awkwardly.

"It could be a girl." he says with narrow eyes. "And that's no excuse, come dance." He offers his hand and I don't refuse. Dancing with my Greek god of a husband? Can't be too bad.

*   *   *

Pete, Kira, Will, Amber, Jacob, Javi, Kaidan and I have all met up for lunch. Everyone is drinking wine except me. Bump is still standing his ground inside of me. Pete and Kira managed to

221

find a babysitter so they don't have Leila with them, granting them an hour of peace.

"I want to make a toast," Jacob pipes up. "My heart is overcome with joy seeing how this friendship has evolved and stood the test of time. It's really true . . . that family isn't always blood." This gets an emotional agreement from everyone. "And Grace, you're going to pop any time soon." He winks. "And that we are all so content in our lives. Seven years down the line and we are all closer than ever. I hope our children will be the same." He coughs and glances down to Javi. "Javi and I actually have an announcement. We have decided to adopt a baby," he says happily, holding Javi's hand. Everyone cheers with excitement and congratulates them.

"The woman is due any day now, so there could be a little baby in the Sanders household for Christmas!" Javi says excitedly, pecking Jacob's cheek. I grin stupidly, before feeling very strange.

Have I just wet myself?

My hand instinctively grasps Kaidan's arm. Oh no. It's happening.

"Gracie, what's wrong?" he asks. All eyes are on me and my eyes are wide.

"My water just broke."

*   *   *

We're all at the hospital in a flash. Everyone came, eager to be present for the birth. The contractions are painful and consistent.

Get out of me, bump!

I'm wheeled through into a single room, leaving all my friends in the waiting area. Kaidan is holding my hand tightly with a contorted look on his face.

You're not the one in labor! I want to say angrily but another contraction rolls through me and I shriek in pain.

222

"Gracie, baby, you've got this," Kaidan says, trying to soothe me. *I've got this? I've got this?* Anger courses through me.

"I am in flipping labor, Kaidan! Of course, I've got this!" I scream in his face. He closes his eyes slowly, probably to stop himself from saying an angry remark back.

"All you did was impregnate me! You don't have to carry this monster inside you and push it out of you!" I shout and see Kaidan exchanging a tired glance with the nurse pushing me.

"Don't you dare side with him," I hiss at the nurse, who gives me a small smile and an apology. Now I understand why women are so angry when they're in labor.

I'm on the bed in a matter of seconds, before everything blurs into pain, shouting, and sweating.

*   *   *

After one last push, the baby is finally out of me. Kaidan did what he was told and stayed by my side, but now he goes to see our baby.

"Congratulations, Mrs. Micah. You have a little boy," the doctor tells me. I sigh in relief. I knew it! They take him away to clean him up and I lie backwards in exhaustion.

"A little boy." Kaidan squeezes my hand and kisses my forehead. "What on earth will we call him?" Kaidan and I decided to not think of names until bump was out of me.

"Bump?" I mumble tiredly, but Kaidan just laughs.

"You know what, Gracie?" he asks.

"Mm?"

"I think we should call him Jared," he says and it silences me. I am in awe of my husband at times. He is so incredibly amazing and loving that I cannot believe he's mine.

"I think you're right, Mr. Micah," I say with a large smile. He grins in reply and gives me a quick peck on the lips.

"I love you, Gracie," he mutters against my lips, and I just nod in reply. The doctor comes back over holding our baby. I cover my mouth in adoration and they place little Jared in my arms. A tear escapes my eyes. He's so cute!

I place a small kiss onto his little face and his eyes are sealed shut in a blissful sleep. I wonder how long that will last…

*   *   *

A crying wakes us. I roll over to face Kaidan, his eyes shut.

"It's your turn," I mumble sleepily. He shakes his head in reluctance.

"If we just leave him, maybe he'll be quiet."

"Kaidan," I whine. "I'm cooking Christmas lunch tomorrow. I think I deserve sleep."

I hear Kaidan sigh before getting out of bed. I smile in victory before closing my eyes again. It takes all of fifteen minutes for Kaidan to make Jared be quiet.

"Thanks," I mumble to Kaidan as he climbs back into bed. He mumbles something incoherent so I quickly place a kiss on his lips.

"I love you." I open my eyes slightly to see a small smile on his face. He can never stay angry at me for too long.

Snow is falling,
All around me,
Children playing,
Having fun.
It's the season,
Love and understanding,
Merry Christmas everyone.

I'm dancing around the kitchen with Jared in my arms. For some Christmas miracle, he didn't wake us up again last night.

224

Kaidan is cooking some sort of Australian Christmas pudding as I prepare the main lunch.

The house is marvelously Christmassy with a large tree, fairy lights, and decorations everywhere. Even little Jared has a smile in his face.

Will and Amber are the first to arrive, each carrying a present. We all wish each other a merry Christmas and Amber smothers Jared entirely. I'm glad, it's good to have him off my hands for once.

Will and Kaidan are chatting about some guy stuff and I just look at my husband adoringly. Javi and Jacob burst in singing Deck the Halls, and Jacob is dressed up as Santa Claus. I grin at him and give him a big hug.

Pete and Kira are last to arrive with little Leila on Kira's hip with a toothless grin. Hugs are given and presents are placed under the tree. What a merry Christmas it will be.

BOOK YOU MIGHT ENJOY

TYLER'S GEM
Rua Hasan

Crystal has always been insecure about being overweight and is constantly being bullied.

When she losses her parents, she leaves the city and her best friend, Matt, behind.

Four years later, Crystal returns with an athletic body.

Is she ready to face everyone and fight back against Tyler–his ultimate bully?

Witness this story of revenge, friendship, and love.

BOOK YOU MIGHT ENJOY

THROUGH YOUR EYES
Ali Merci

Carmen West likes to paint.

Art, she believes, makes up for the lack of light in her. Even if it comes in the form of a boy who carries the sun in his eyes.

Asa San Román is afraid his looks are all that he'll be liked for.

He's reckless, sometimes hotheaded, incredibly passionate and likes to drown him-self in whatever takes the insecurities away.

Carmen is satisfied living with her heart under wraps, but then she meets Asa, who wears his on his sleeve—and he reminds her that even after the darkest of nights, comes the breaking of light.

Asa is fine with trying to erase parts of his identity, but then she meets Carmen, the girl with midnight hair and thundercloud eyes—who teaches him that beauty doesn't lie in the colour of his skin, but runs soul-deep instead.

Asa and Carmen fall into place beside each other like two halves of a jigsaw puzzle—perfectly into place.

But then one of them embarks on a journey of self-love while the other still struggles to admit they have too many open wounds that need healing.

And when two people, regardless of the intensity of their feelings, are in complete-ly different points of their lives…

…is love really enough?

ACKNOWLEDGEMENTS

If I'd told my seventeen-year-old self that in five years I would have a published a book, she wouldn't believe me. I can hardly believe it now.

Sweet Revenge was the first book that I ever finished writing, and I am thankful to all the people who helped me on this amazing journey.

To my family: who put up with my insistent demand that one day I WILL be an author. A big shout out to Amelie, who I'd force to read my books, no matter how good they were.

I'd also like to thank my incredible editor, Lyndon. We did it! My book couldn't have turned into what it is now without you. I'd also like to thank you for your patience—when I was stranded in Asia with no WiFi, no laptop, and no way to edit, you were brilliant.

A big thank you to everyone from Typewriter Pub that helped me on my journey, including Michelle, AJ, and finally Bea. You guys rock.

And finally, a big thank you to you, reader. I really hope you enjoyed reading the book as much as I enjoyed writing it.

AUTHOR'S NOTE

Thank you so much for reading *Sweet Revenge*! I can't express how grateful I am for reading something that was once just a thought inside my head.

Please feel free to send me an email. Just know that my publisher filters these emails. Good news is always welcome.
flora_mcconnell@awesomeauthors.org

One last thing: I'd love to hear your thoughts on the book. Please leave a review on Amazon or Goodreads because I just love reading your comments and getting to know you!

Can't wait to hear from you!

Flora McConnell

ABOUT THE AUTHOR

Flora McConnell is a recent graduate from the University of Exeter, where she studied Psychology. She lives in East Sussex with her family and two dogs and eight alpacas. She has enjoyed writing since she was a child, and is the author of the book 'Sweet Revenge' which gained its popularity via the writing platform Wattpad.

Printed in Great Britain
by Amazon

62927249R00142